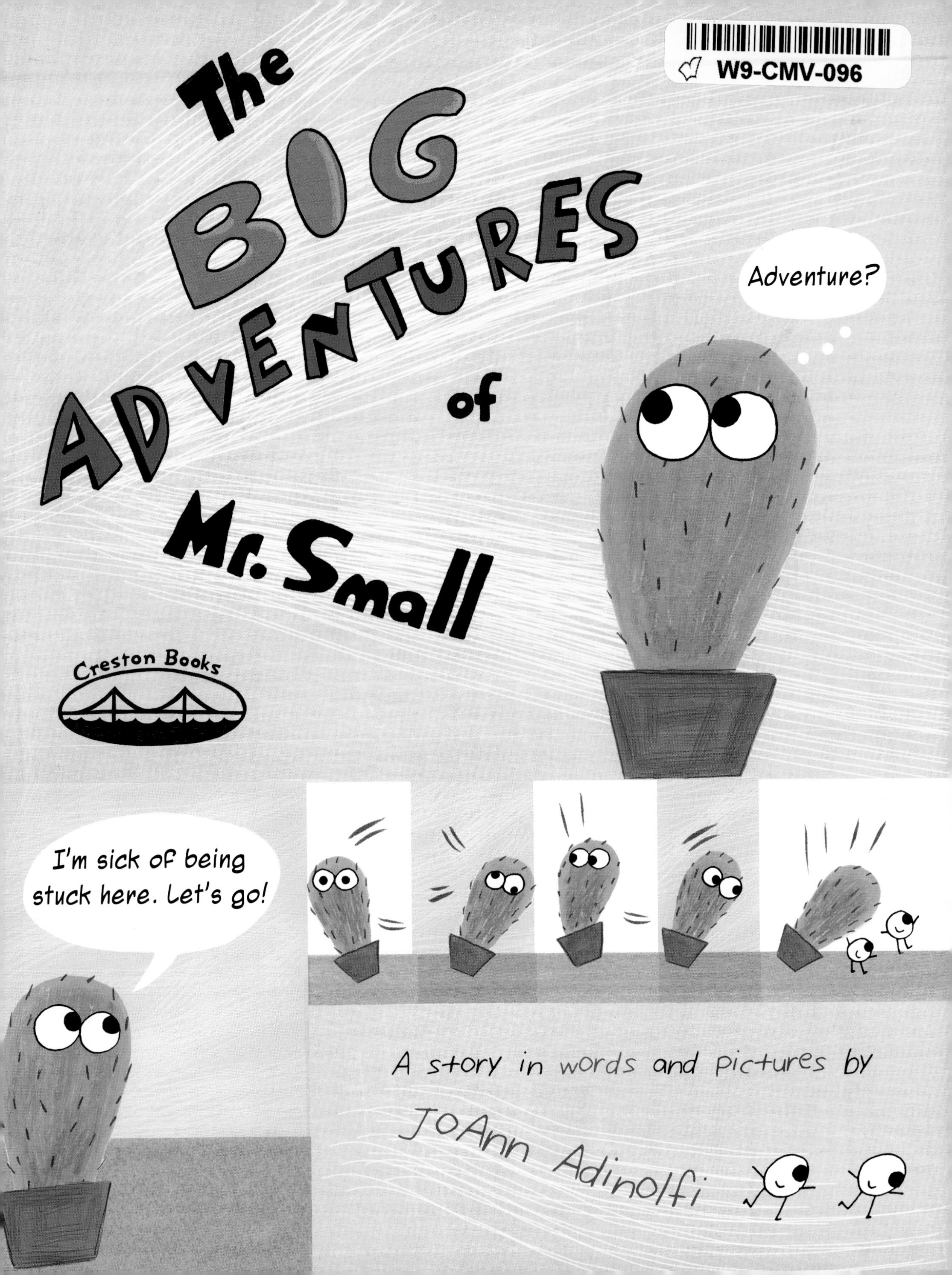
The BIG ADVENTURES of Mr. Small
Adventure?
Creston Books
I'm sick of being stuck here. Let's go!
A story in words and pictures by
JoAnn Adinolfi

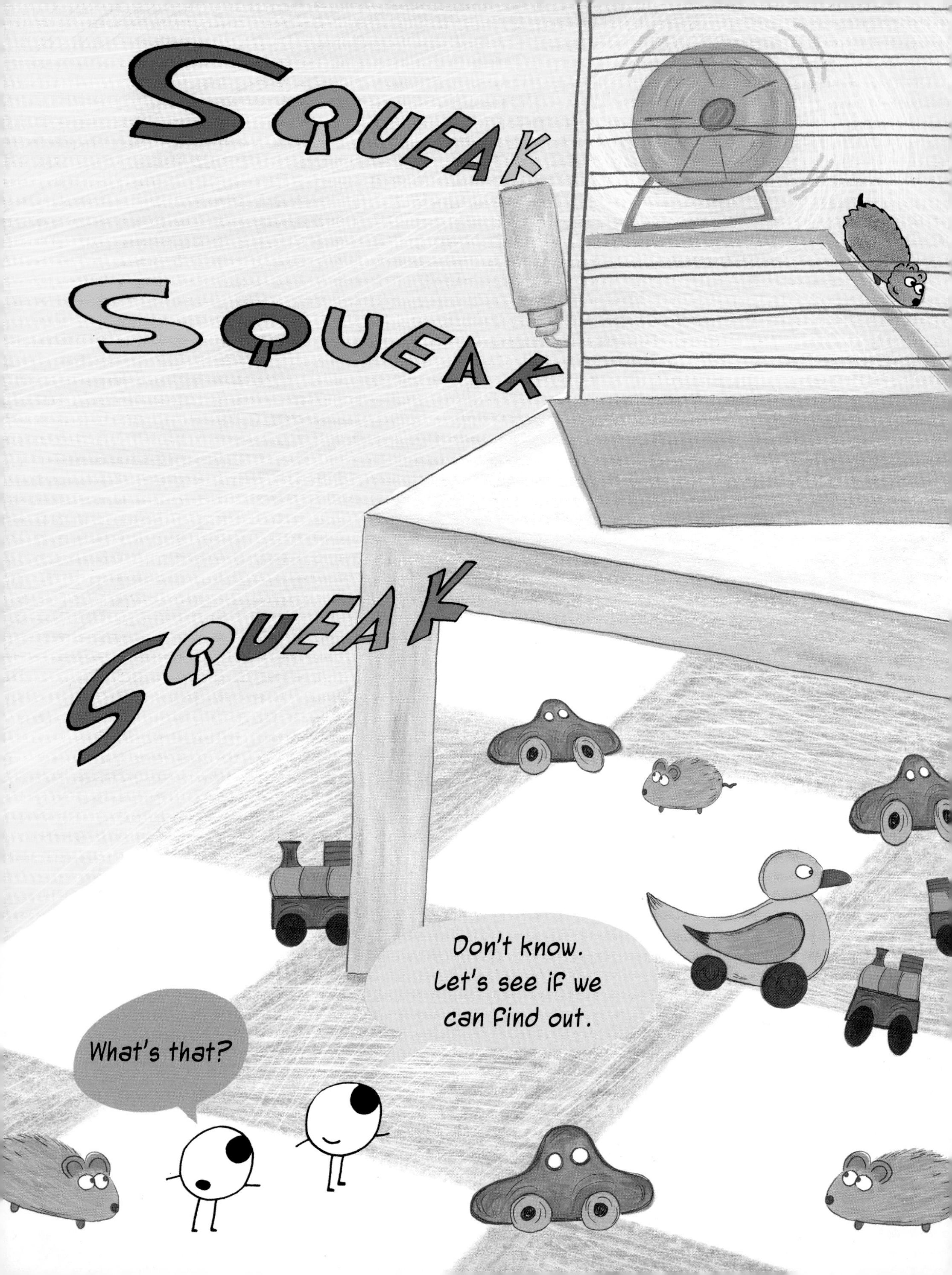
SQUEAK
SQUEAK
SQUEAK
What's that?
Don't know. Let's see if we can find out.

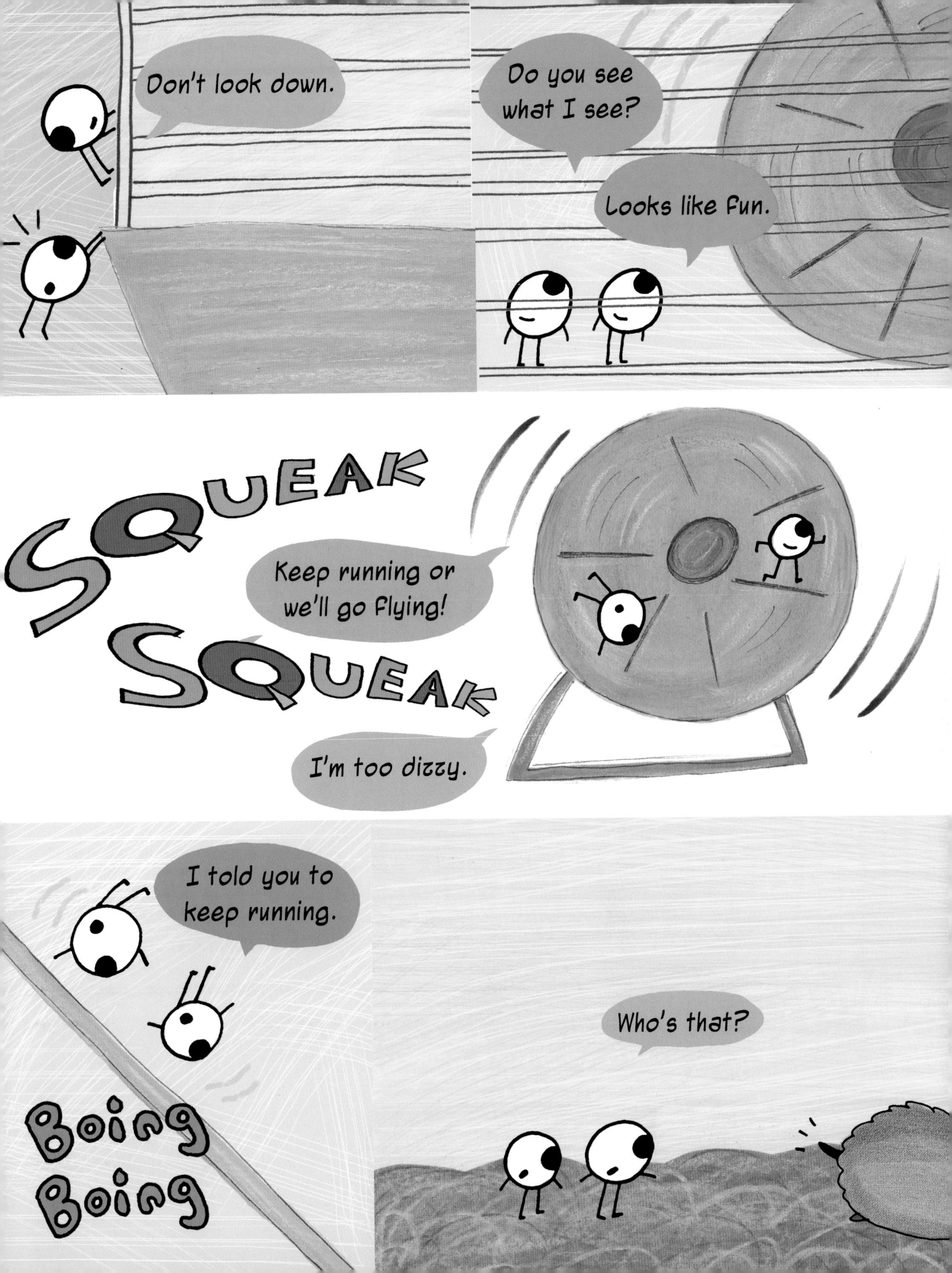
Don't look down.
Do you see what I see?
Looks like fun.
SQUEAK
SQUEAK
Keep running or we'll go flying!
I'm too dizzy.
I told you to keep running.
Boing
Boing
Who's that?

This is Mr. Small.

He is a teeny tiny hamster.

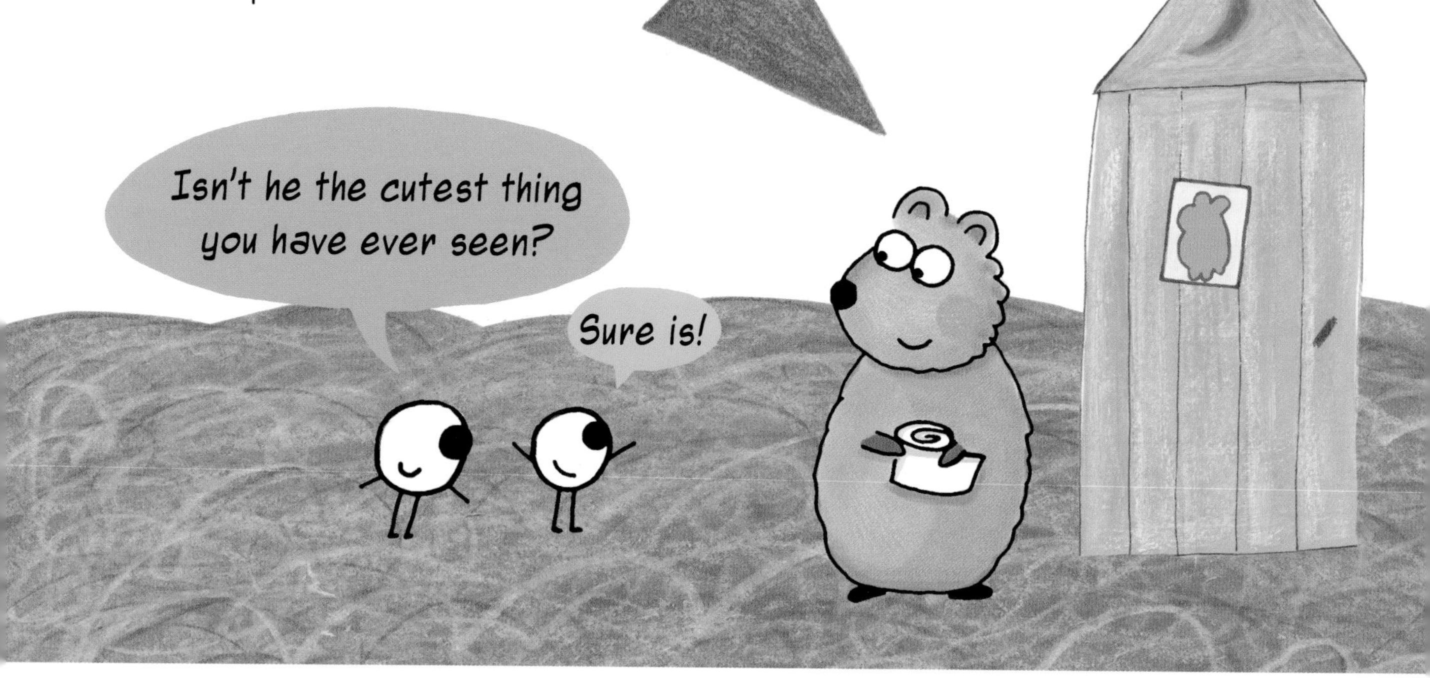
Isn't he the cutest thing you have ever seen?
Sure is!

He likes to stuff his cheeks with food and fluff...

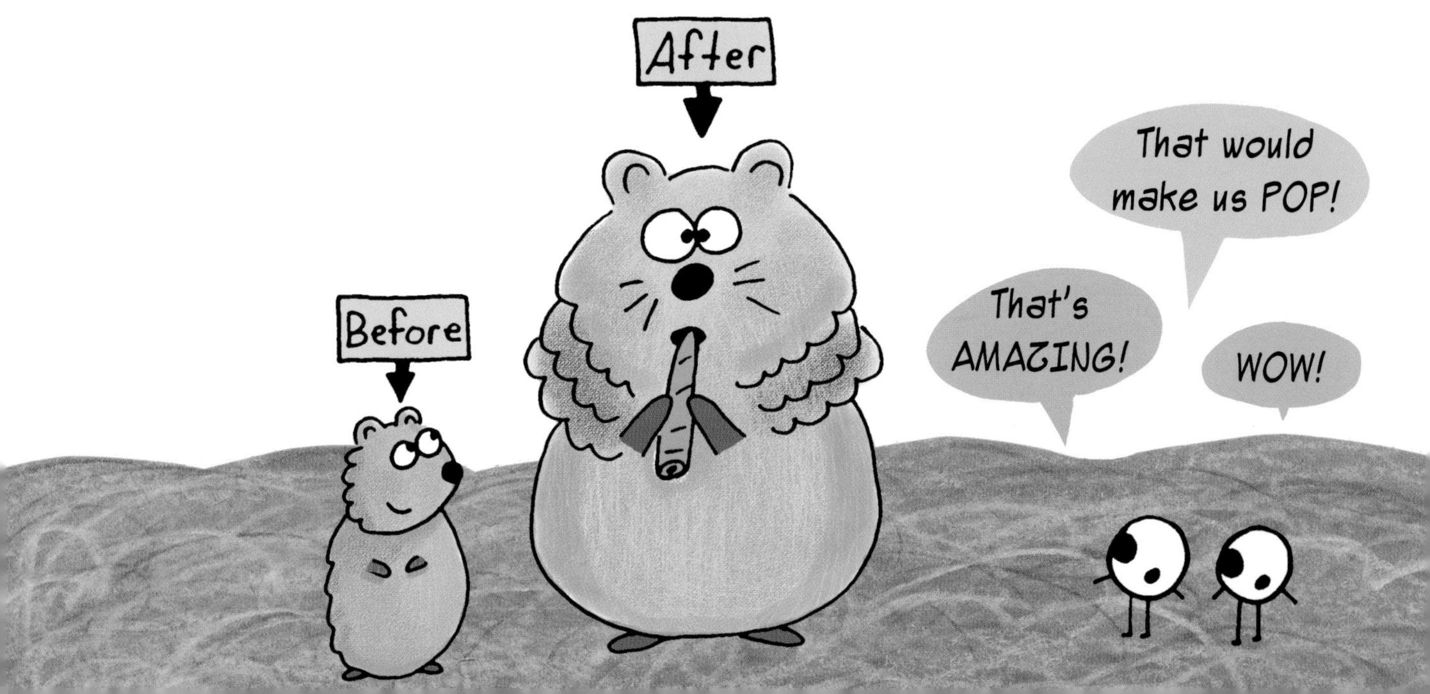
After
Before
That would make us POP!
That's AMAZING!
WOW!

...and put everything into his little house.

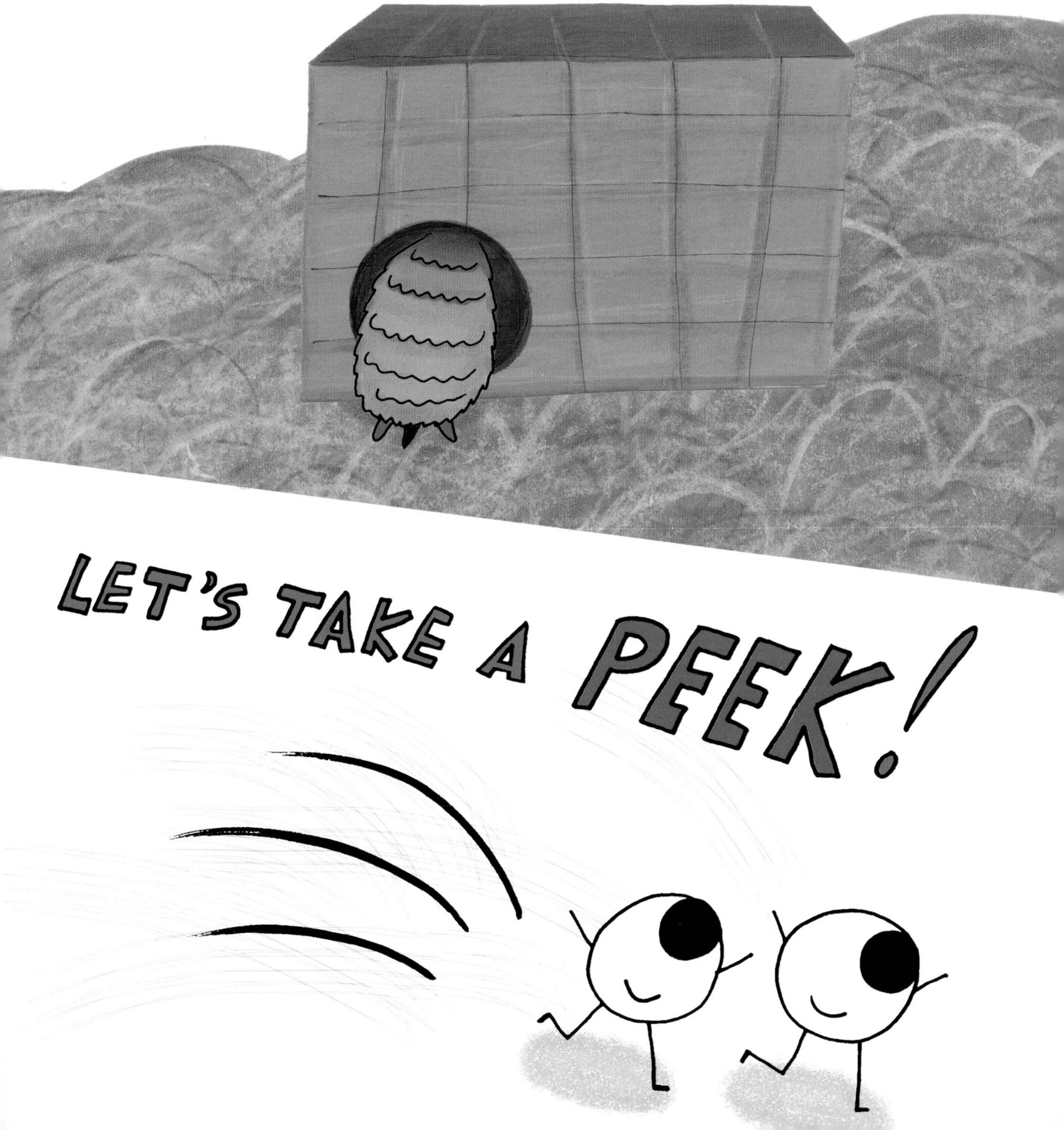
LET'S TAKE A PEEK!

Mr. Small's house is cozy and fluffy and something yummy to eat is never far away.

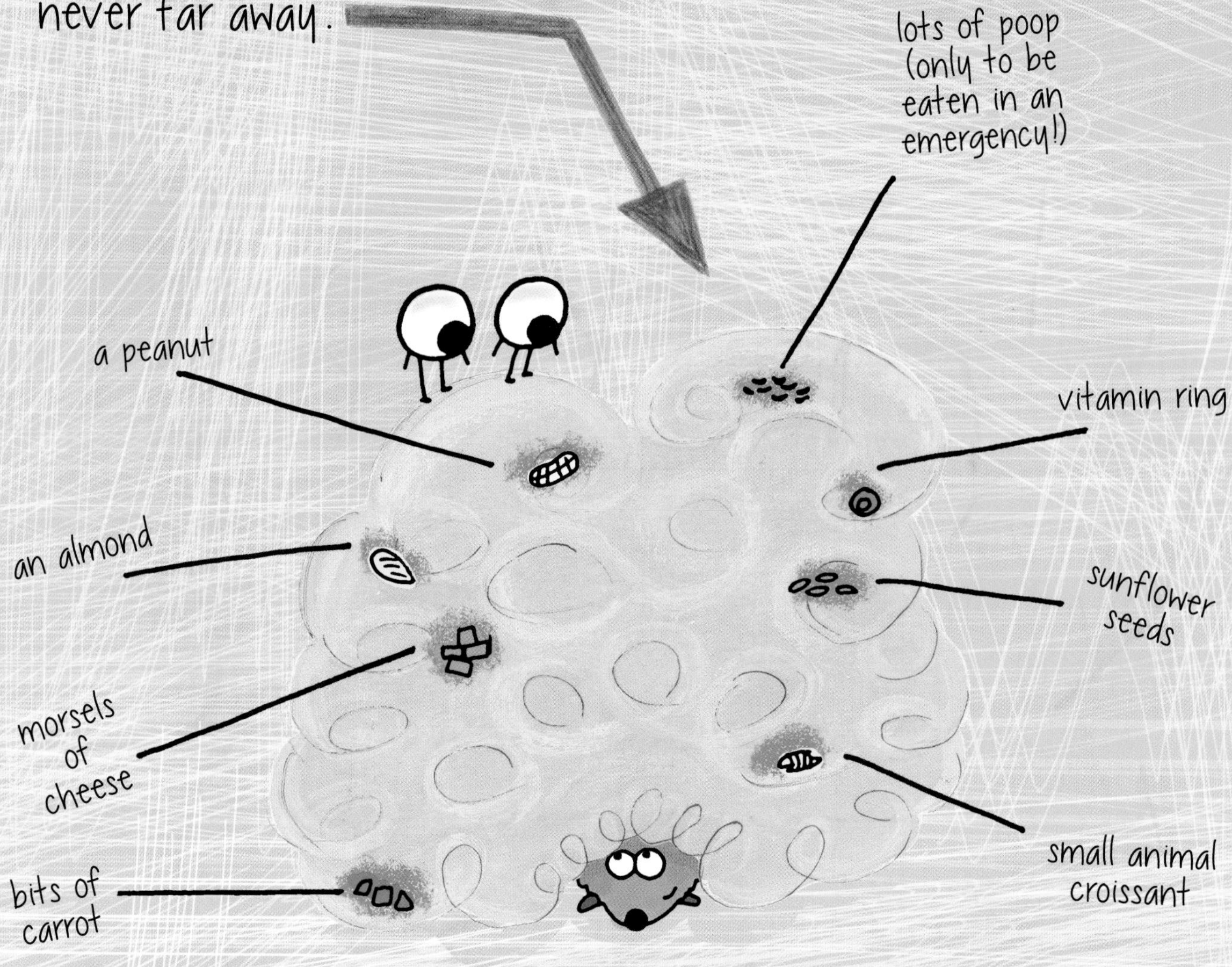
lots of poop (only to be eaten in an emergency!)
a peanut
vitamin ring
an almond
sunflower seeds
morsels of cheese
small animal croissant
bits of carrot

He even has a little light.

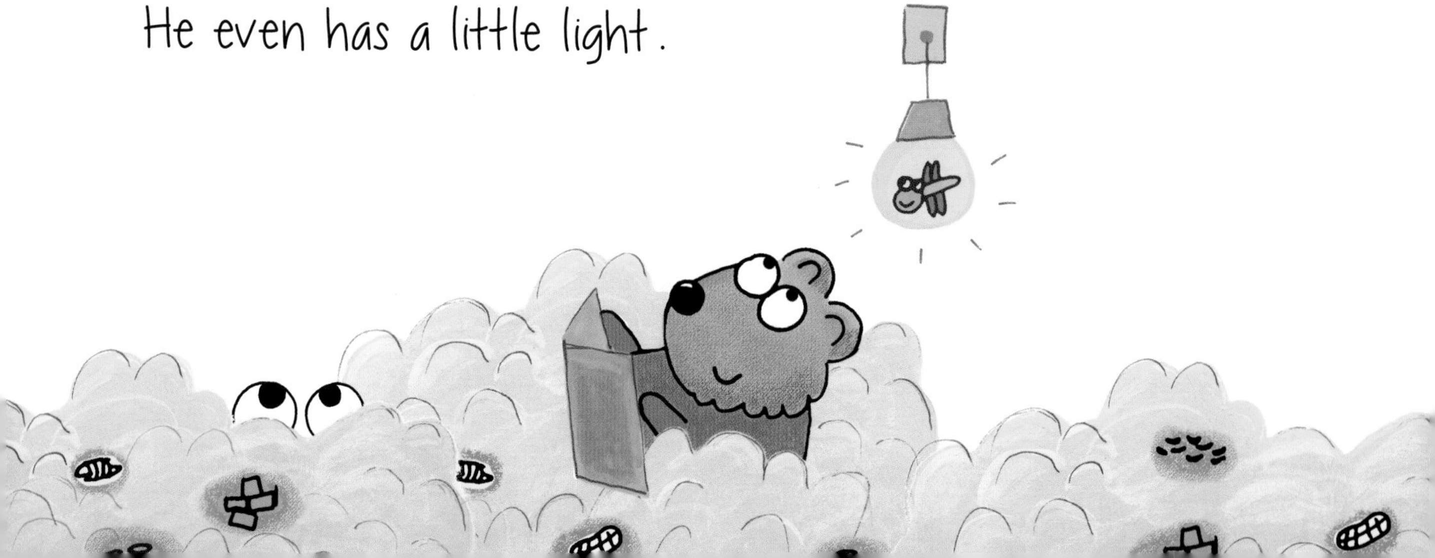

Mr. Small has everything he could possibly need.

What could it be?

EXCEPT...

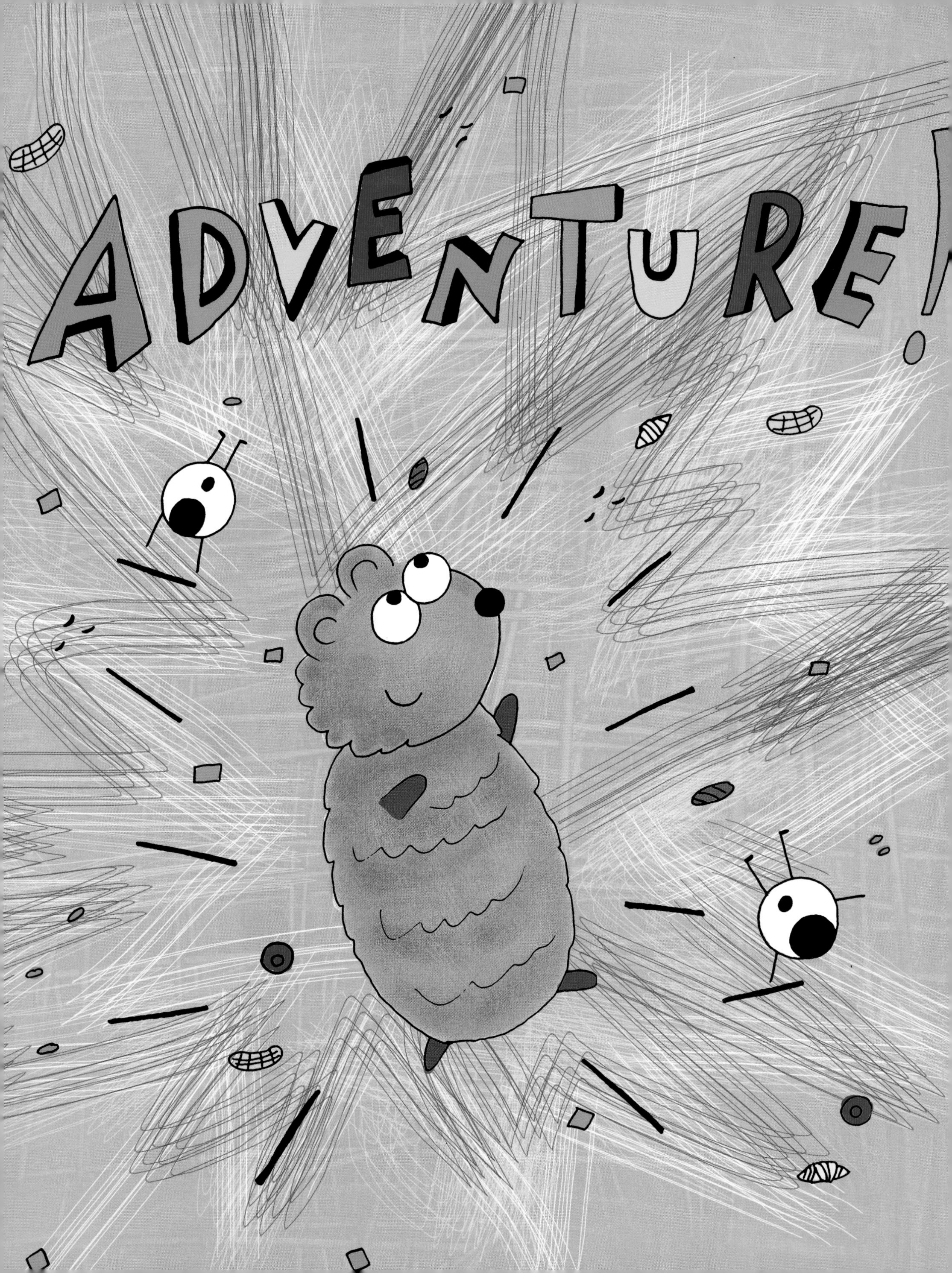
ADVENTURE!

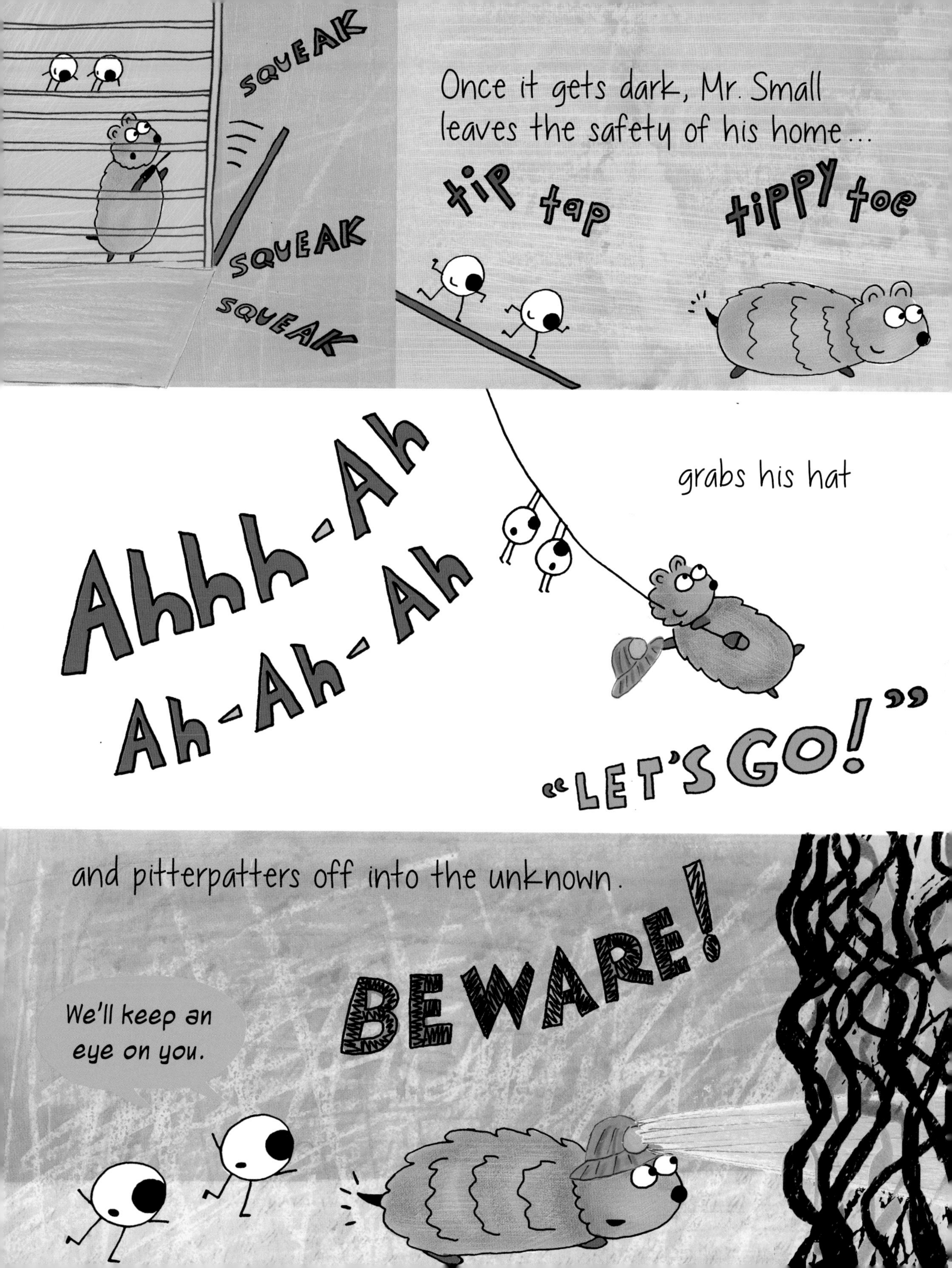
SQUEAK
SQUEAK
SQUEAK
Once it gets dark, Mr. Small leaves the safety of his home...
tip tap
tippy toe
Ahhh-Ah Ah-Ah-Ah
grabs his hat
"LET'S GO!"
and pitterpatters off into the unknown.
We'll keep an eye on you.
BEWARE!

Mr. Small is so little,
yet so brave.
Look out below!

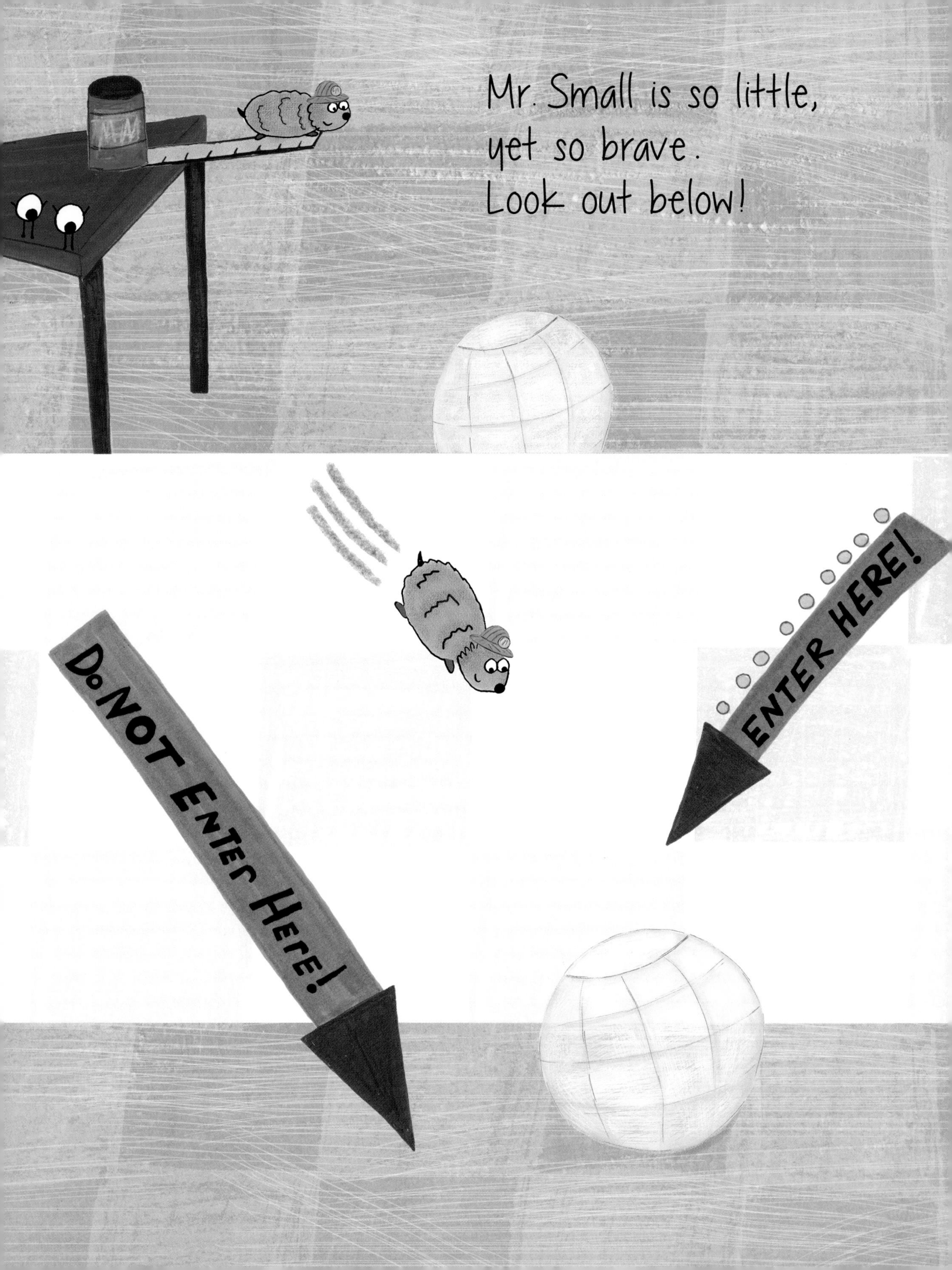
Do NOT Enter Here!
ENTER HERE!

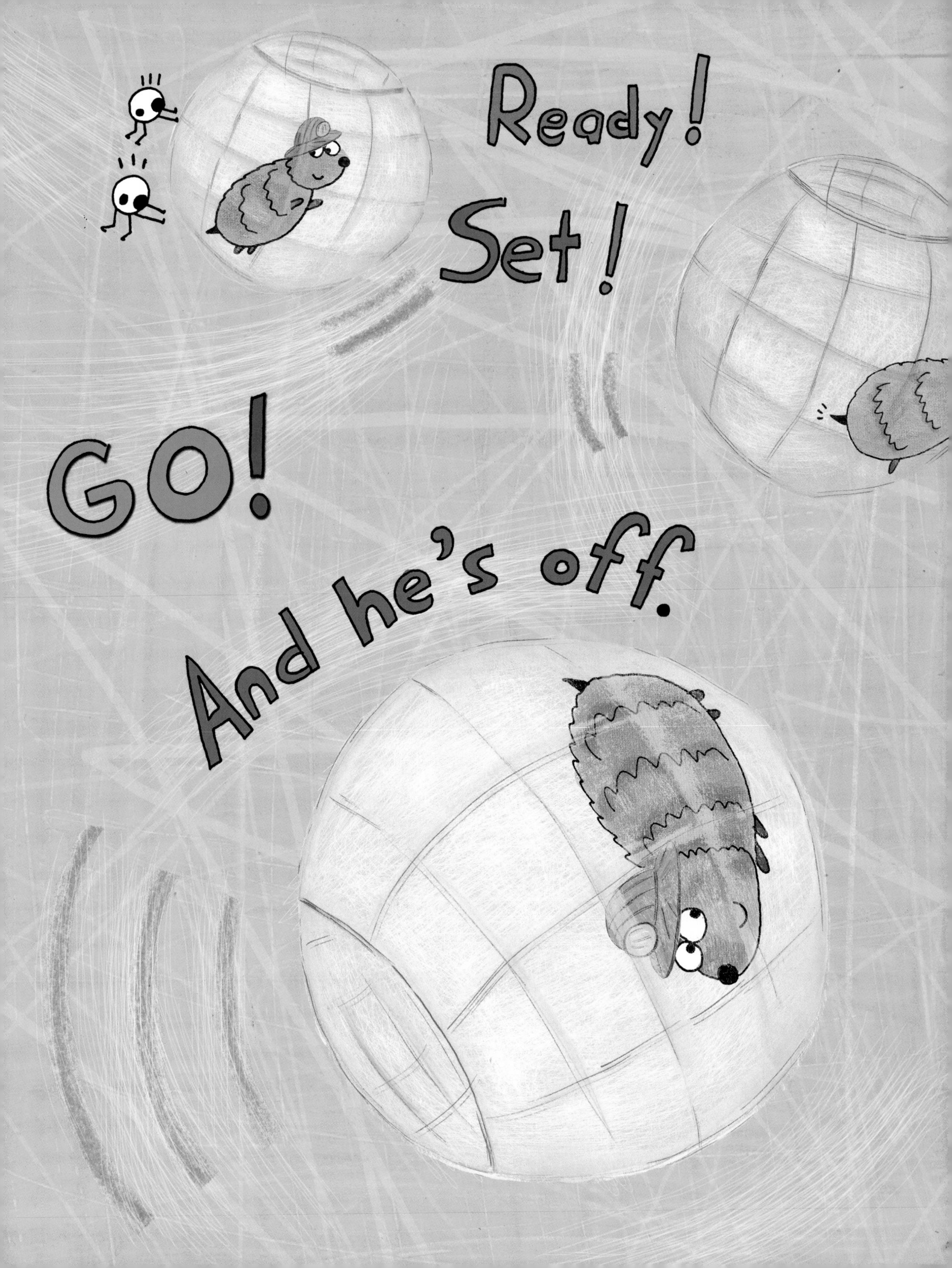
Ready!
Set!
GO!
And he's off.

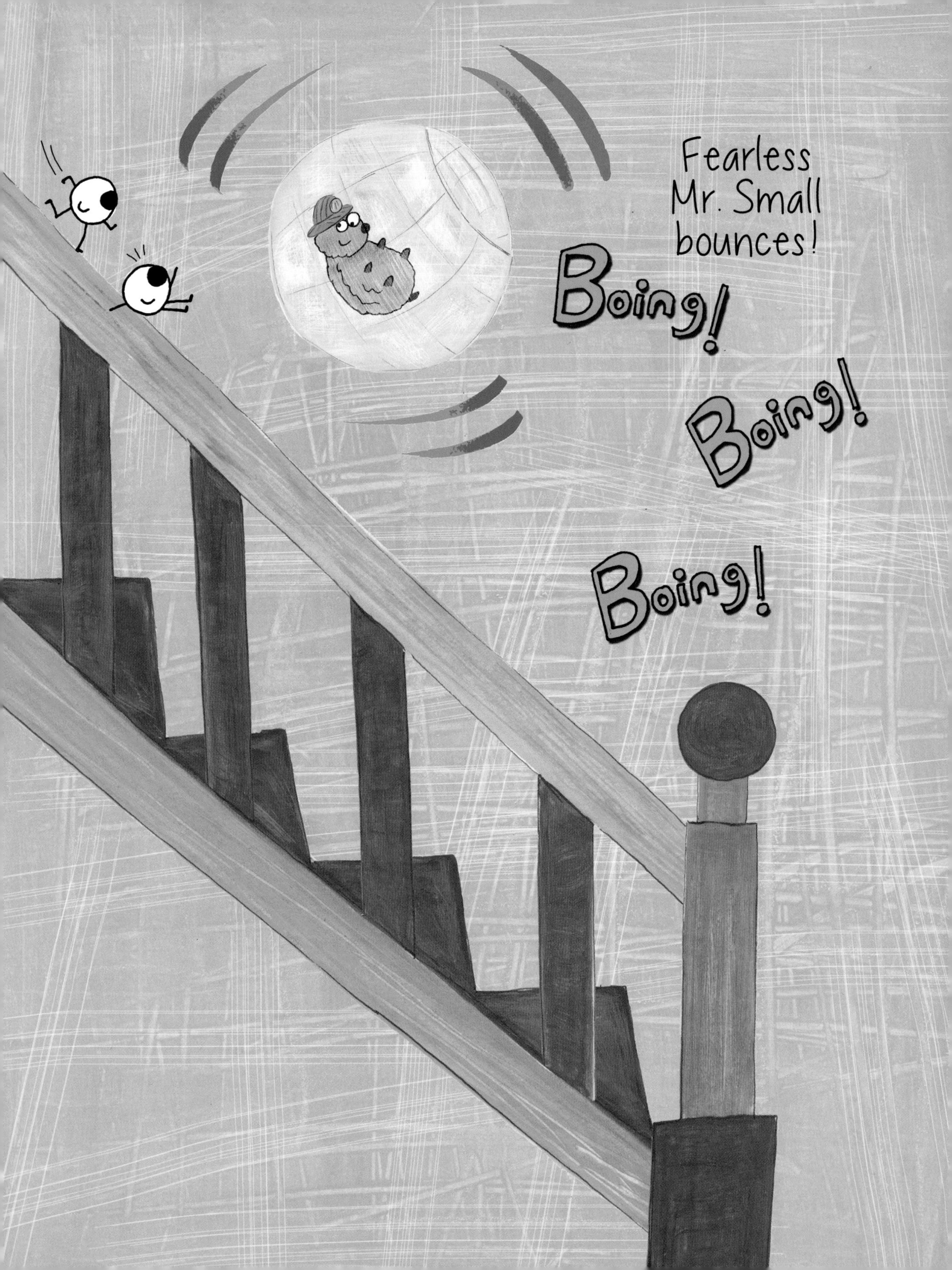
Fearless Mr. Small bounces!
Boing!
Boing!
Boing!

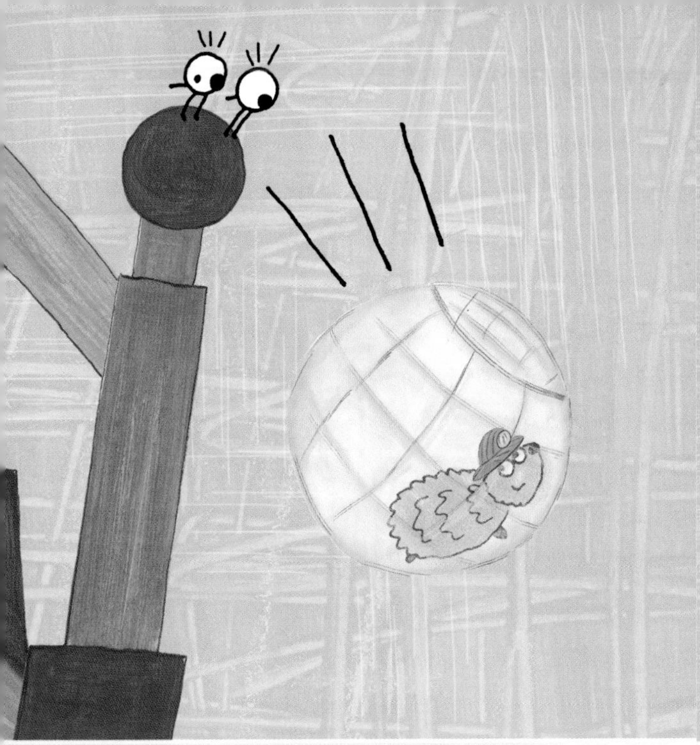

He crashes!

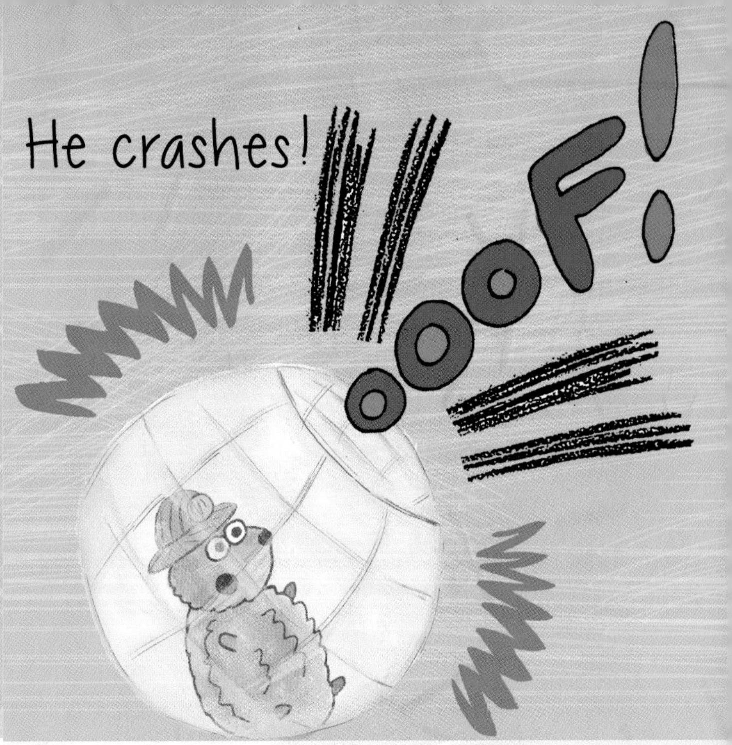
OOOF!

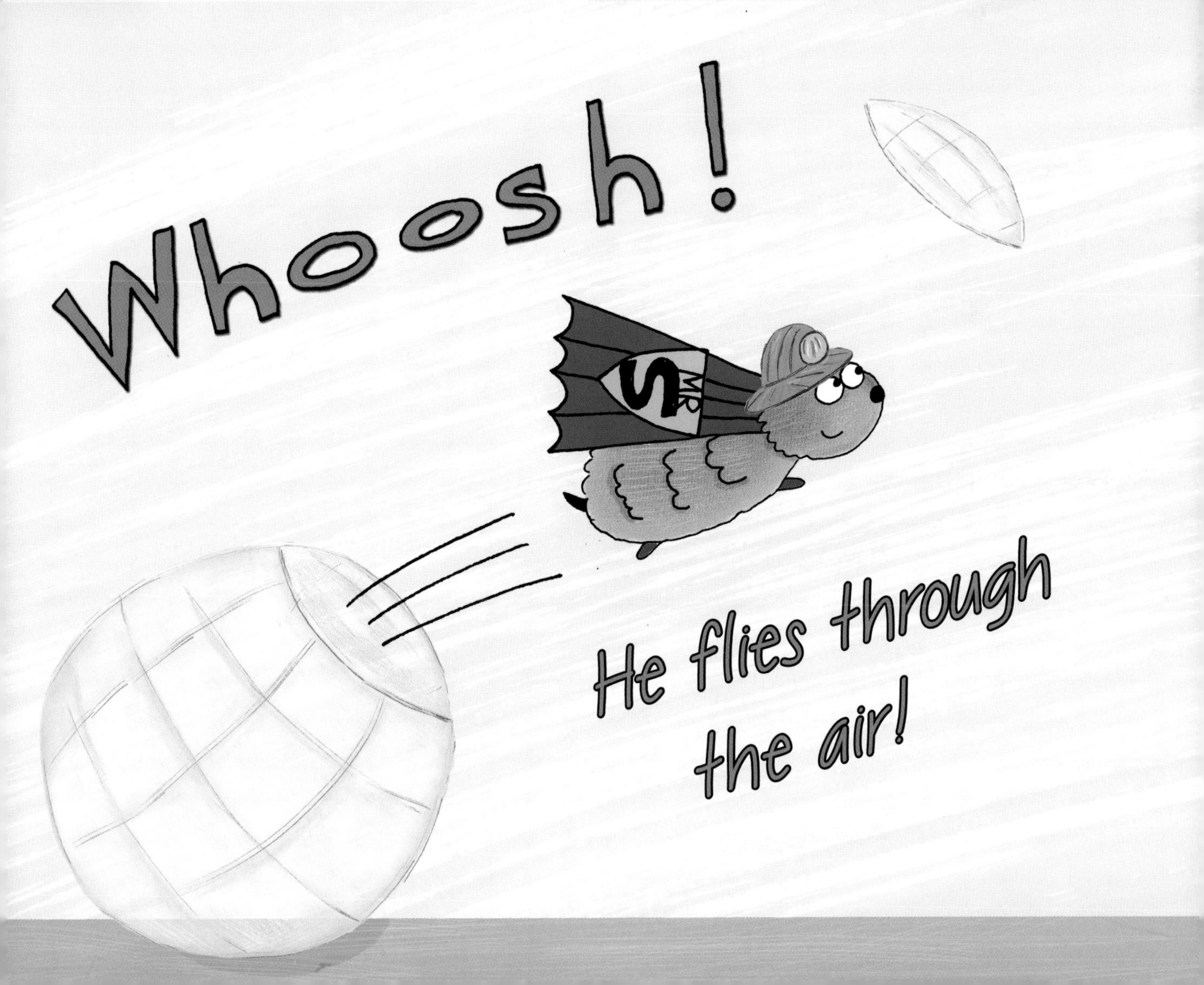
Whoosh!

He flies through the air!

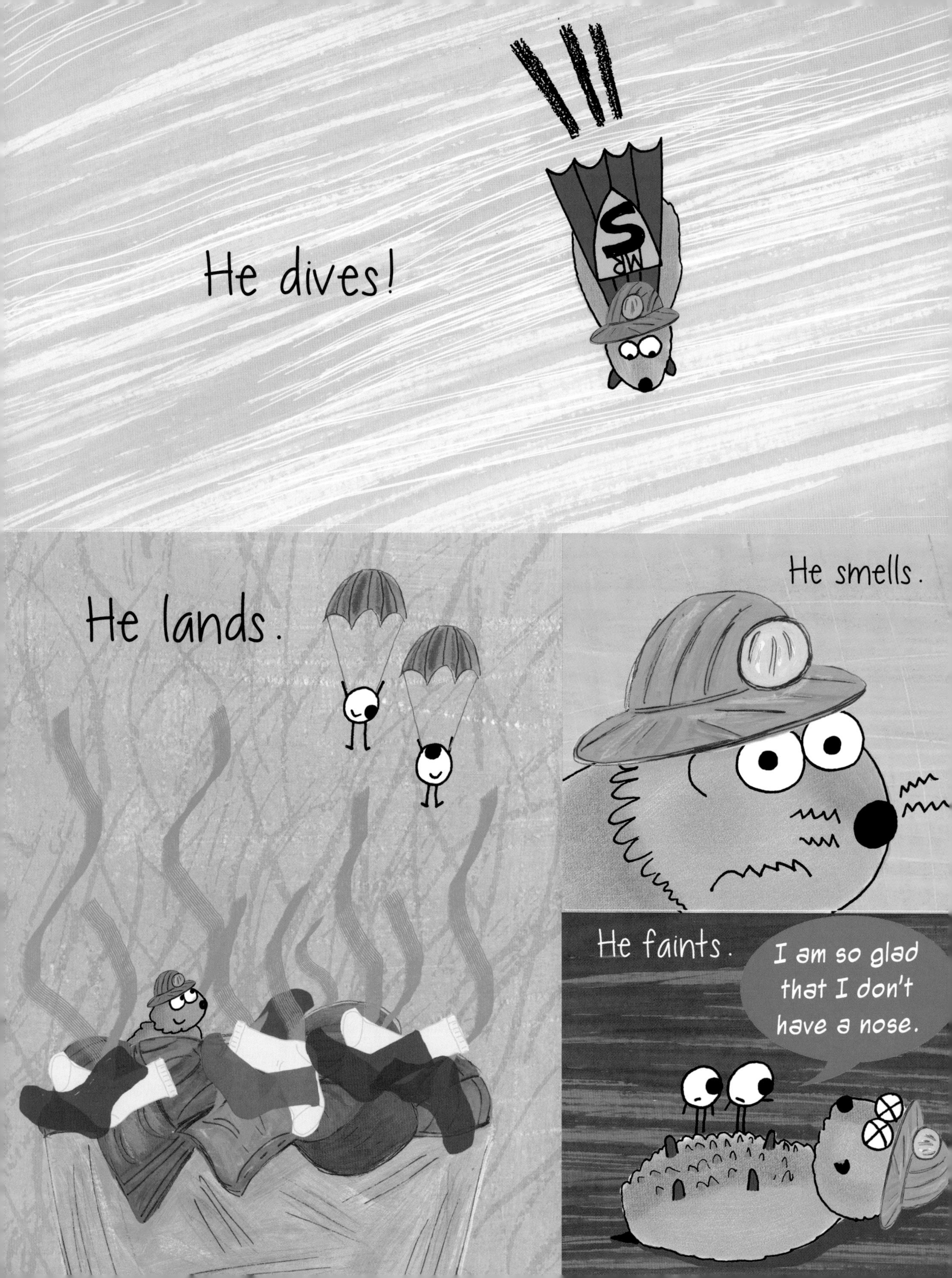
He dives!
He lands.
He smells.
He faints.
I am so glad that I don't have a nose.

He wakes. He scurries.
What's this? ***Oh no!***
It's the living room rug!

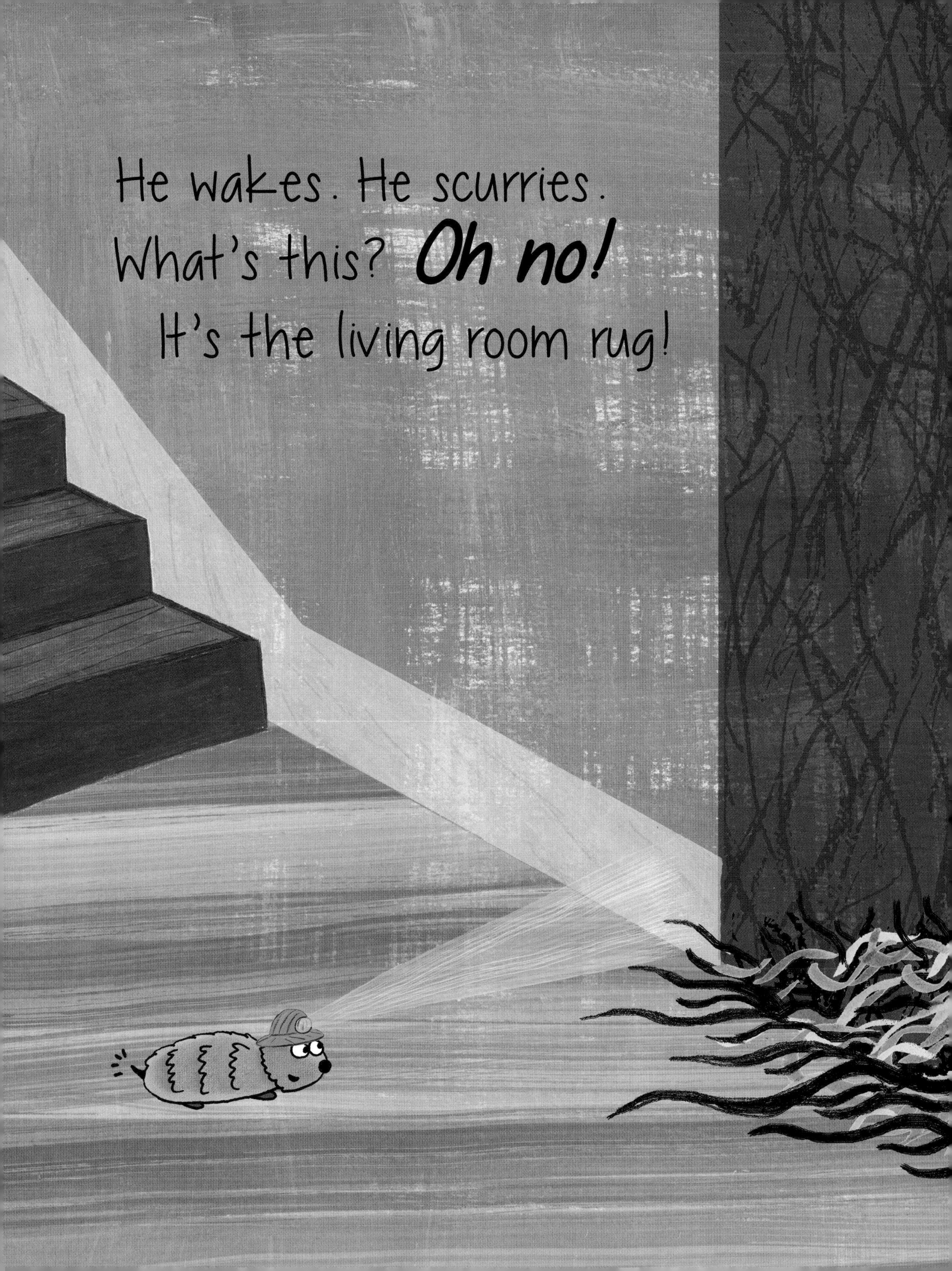

A little hamster like Mr. Small can't find his way through such a thick, furry maze alone. He needs your help.

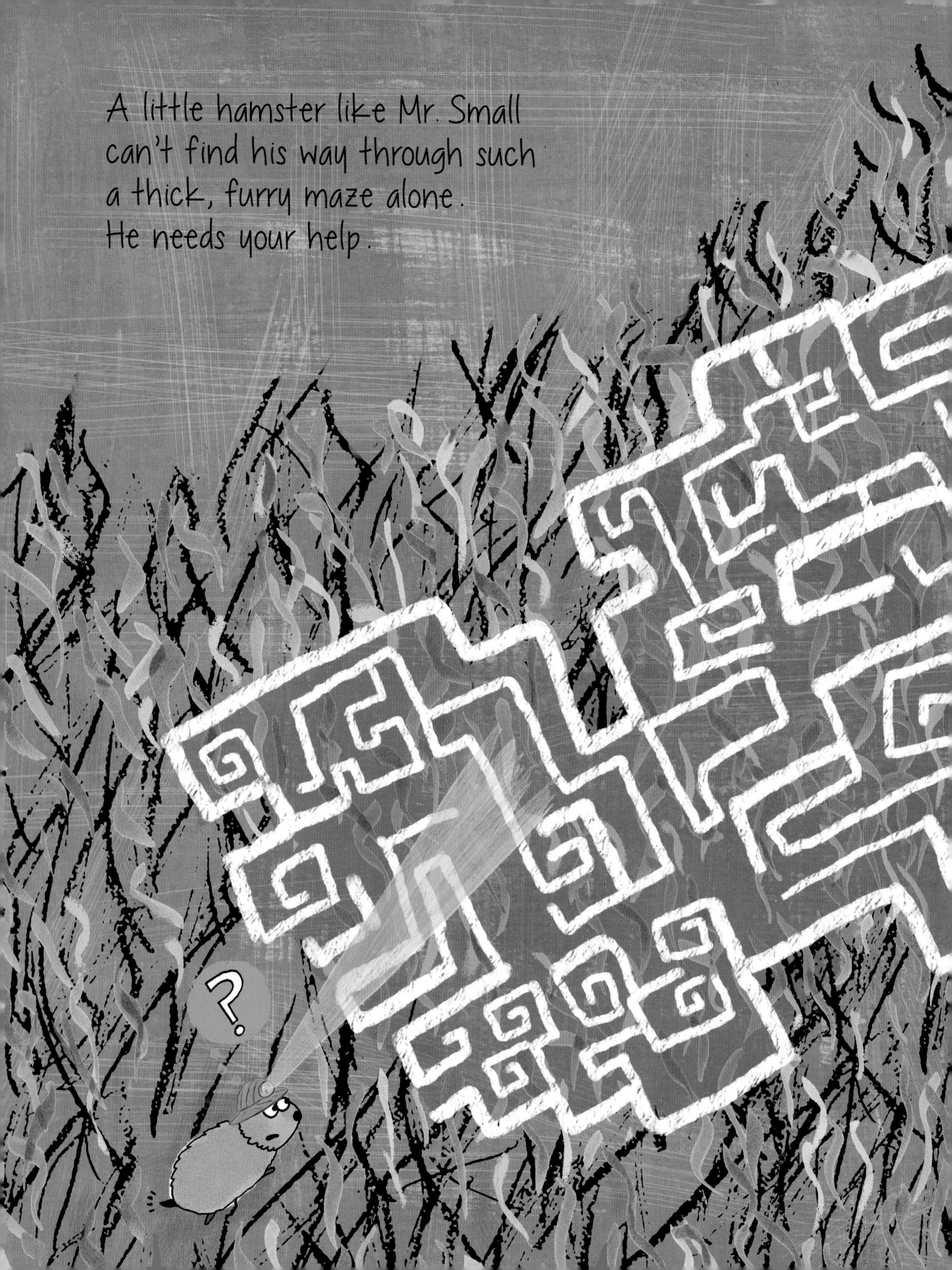

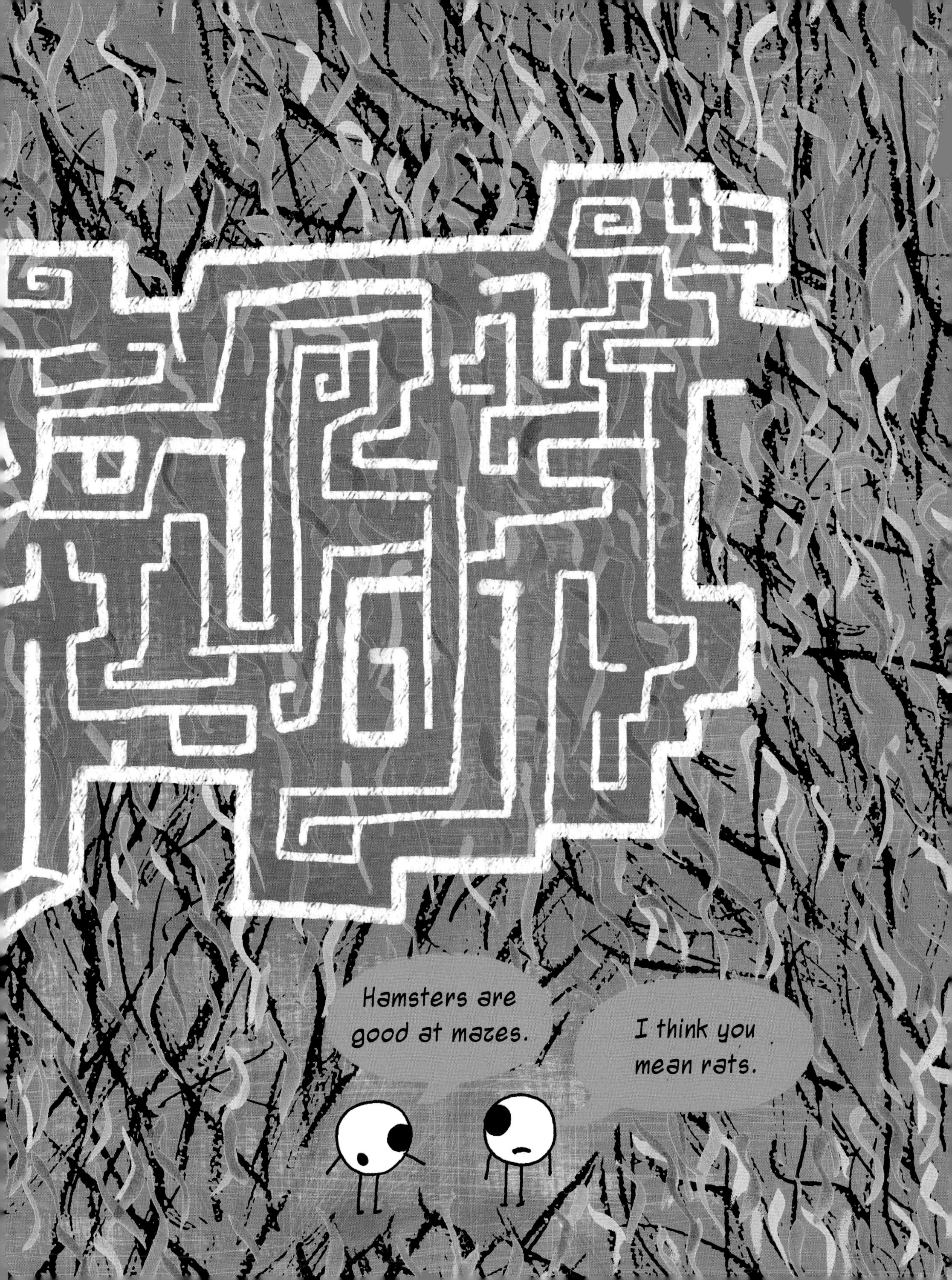
Hamsters are good at mazes.
I think you mean rats.

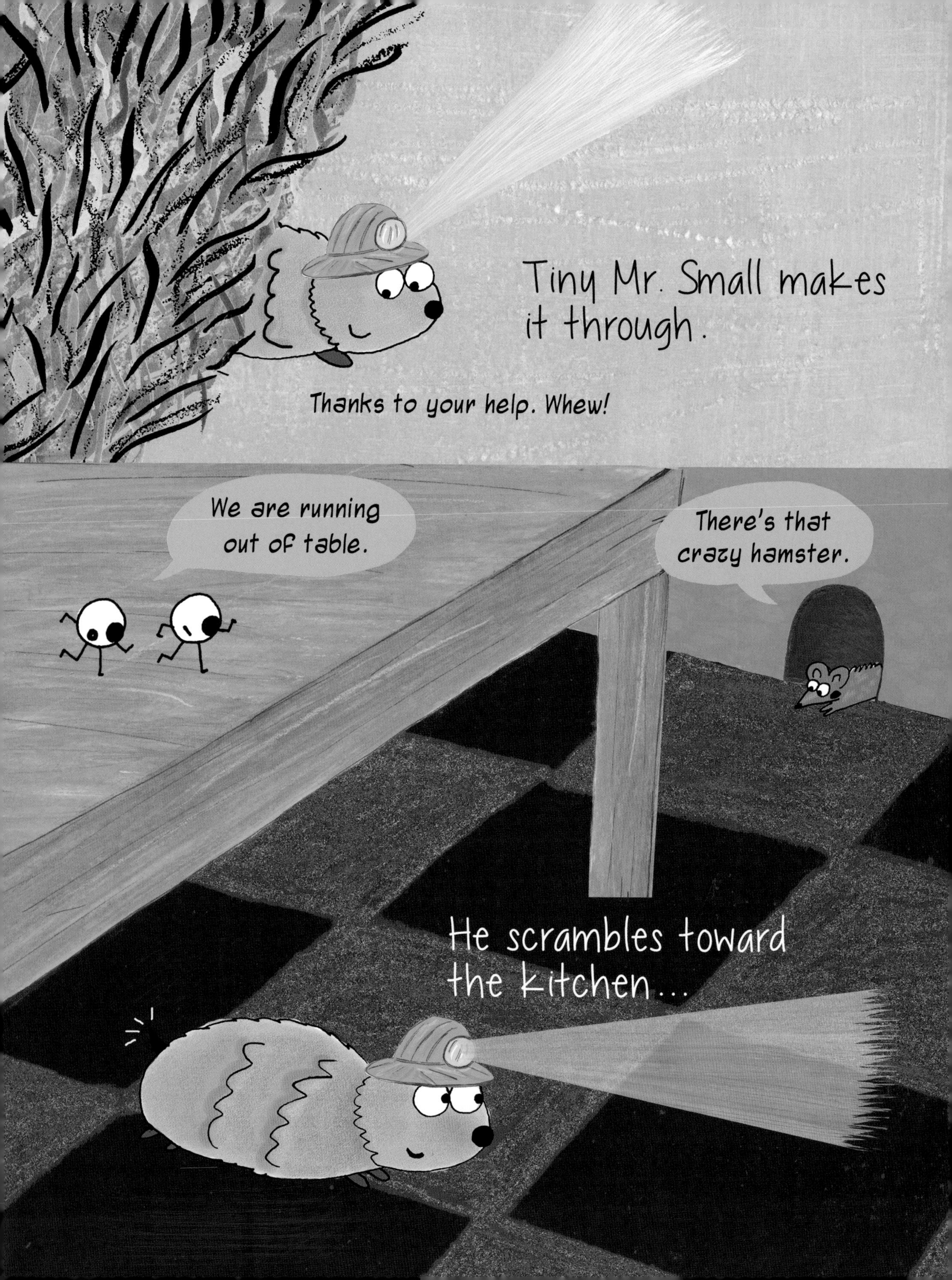
Tiny Mr. Small makes it through.
Thanks to your help. Whew!
We are running out of table.
There's that crazy hamster.
He scrambles toward the kitchen...

……………and under the refrigerator, where it is dark and dusty and…

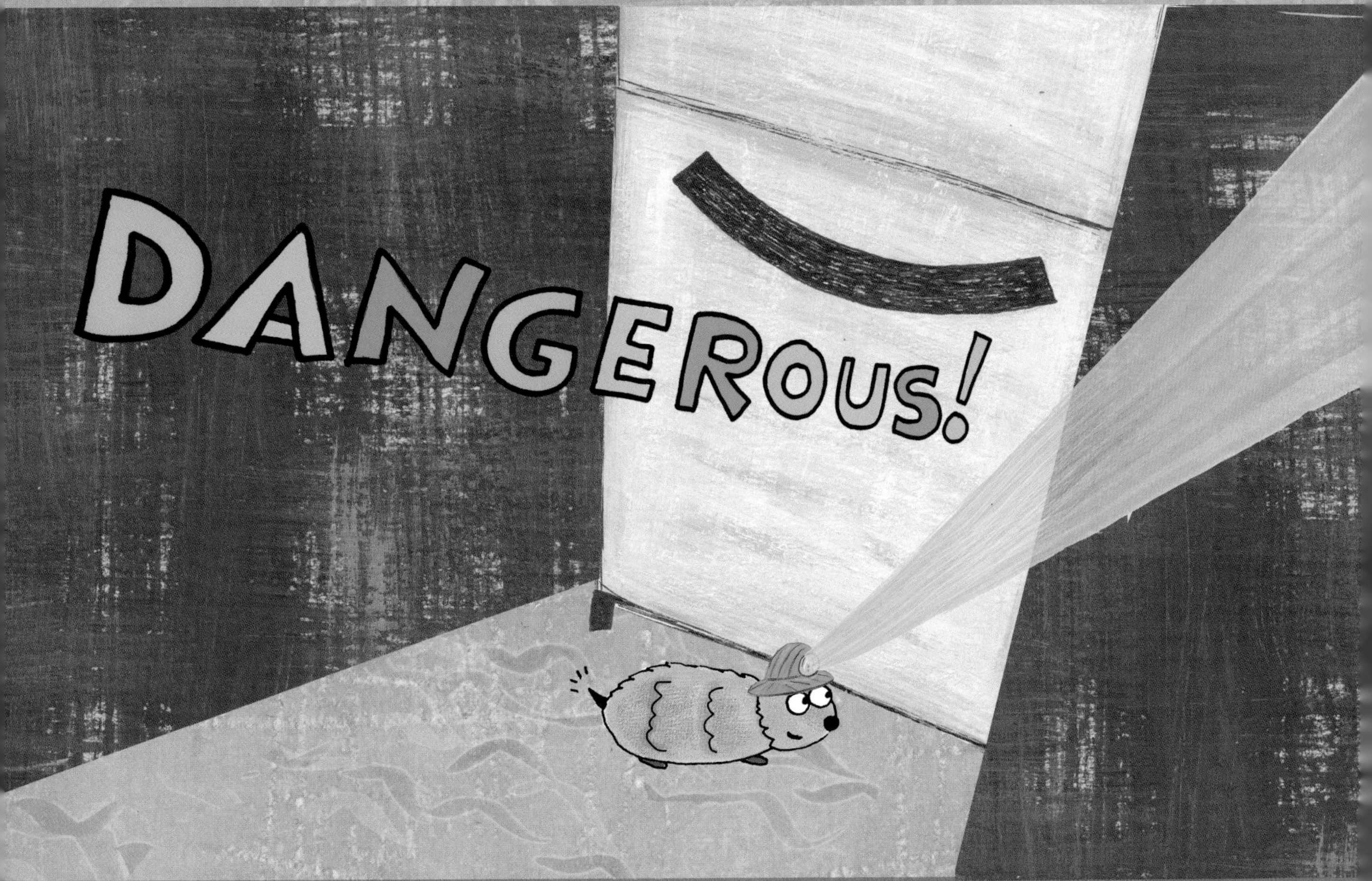
DANGEROUS!

What could Mr. Small dare to find in this forbidden place? With his little paws he creeps deep into peril and exclaims…

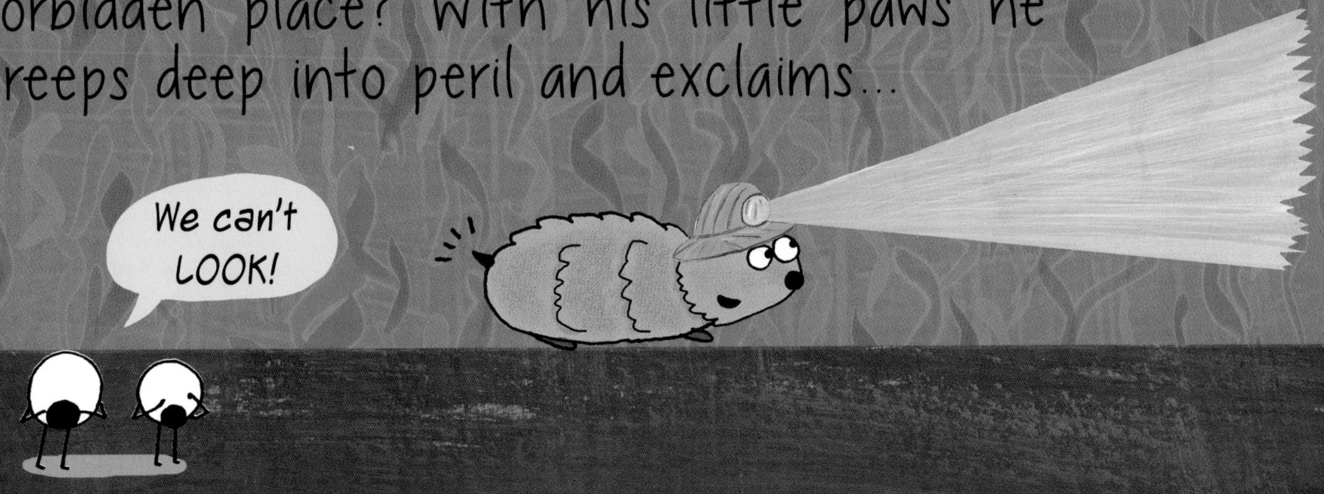
We can't LOOK!

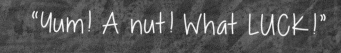

"Yum! A nut! What LUCK!"

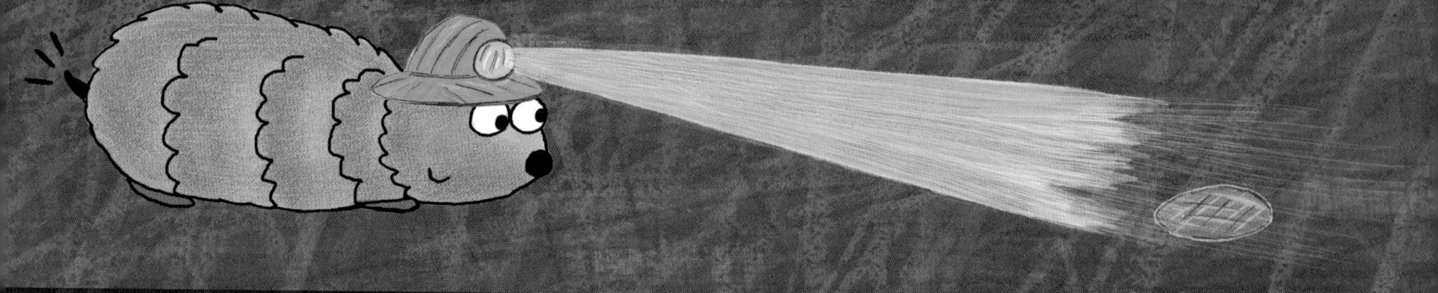

"Don't move a muscle!" a voice squeaks. "That's mine. Move away slowly and you won't get hurt."

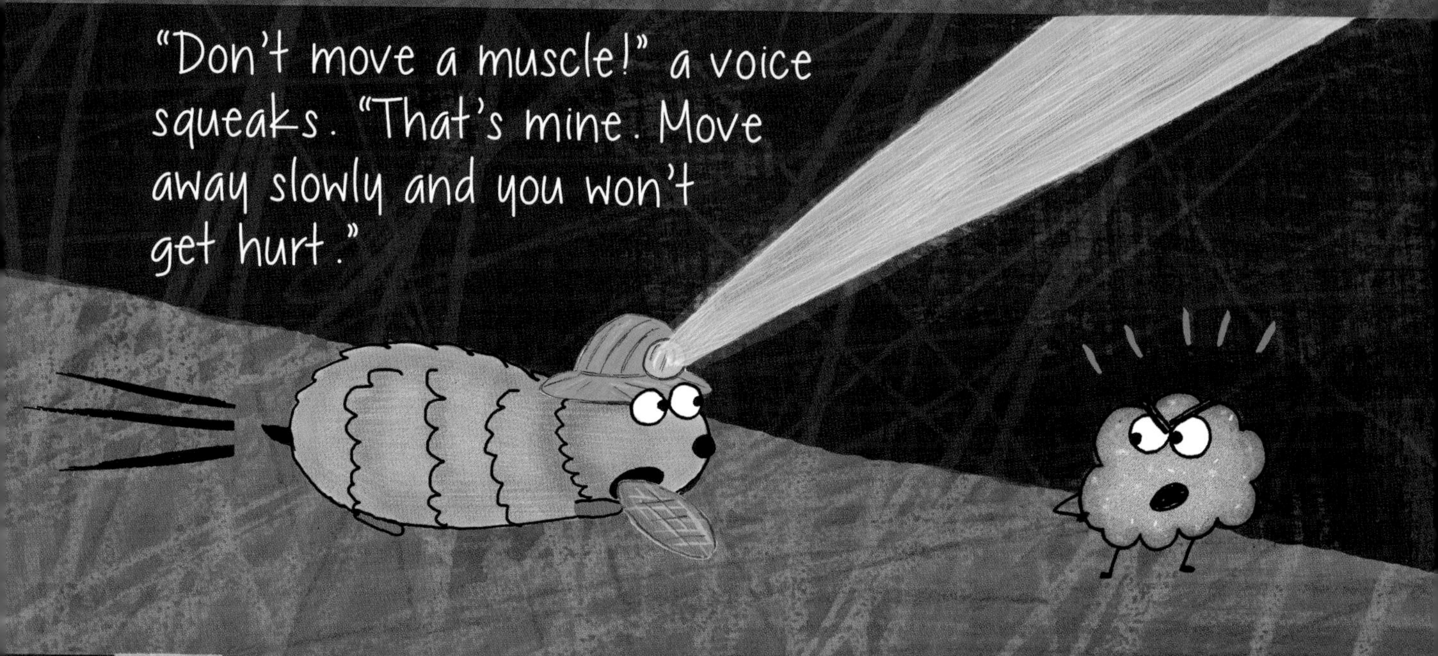

"You are a harmless dust bunny," says Mr. Small.
"That's what you think!" barks the dust bunny.
"You don't want to mess with me!"
"Who are you?" asks Mr. Small.

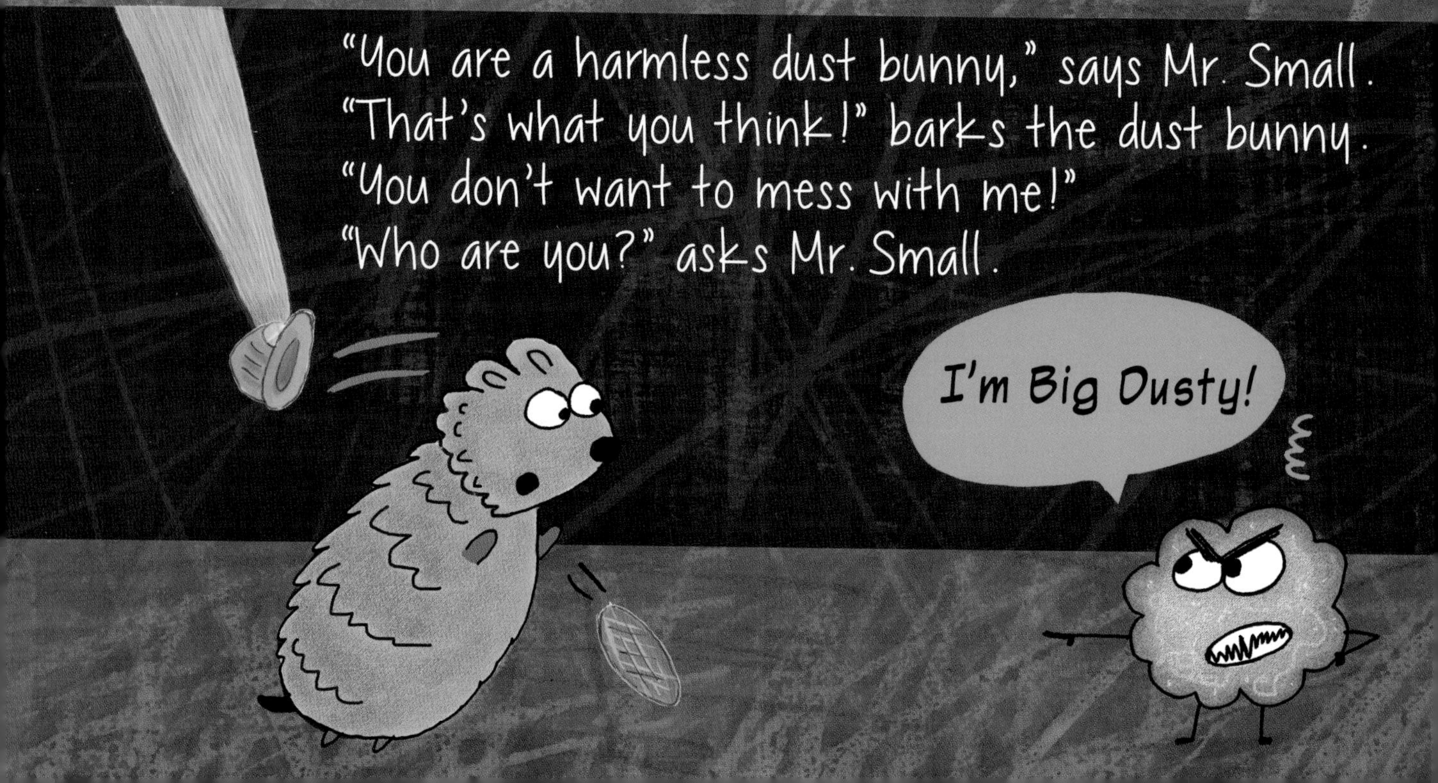
I'm Big Dusty!

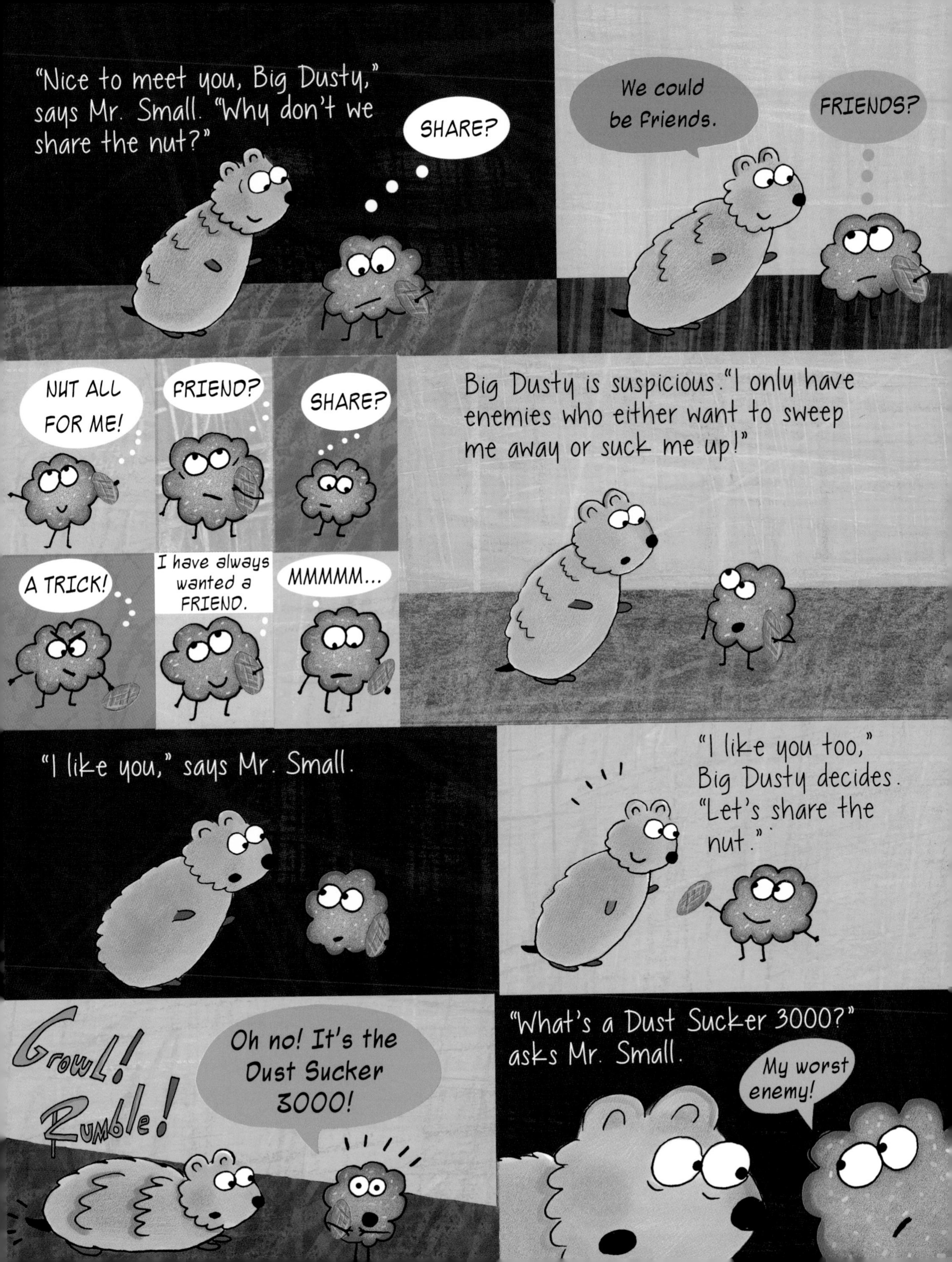
"Nice to meet you, Big Dusty," says Mr. Small. "Why don't we share the nut?"
SHARE?
We could be friends.
FRIENDS?
NUT ALL FOR ME!
FRIEND?
SHARE?
A TRICK!
I have always wanted a FRIEND.
MMMMM...
Big Dusty is suspicious. "I only have enemies who either want to sweep me away or suck me up!"
"I like you," says Mr. Small.
"I like you too," Big Dusty decides. "Let's share the nut."
Growl!
Rumble!
Oh no! It's the Dust Sucker 3000!
"What's a Dust Sucker 3000?" asks Mr. Small.
My worst enemy!

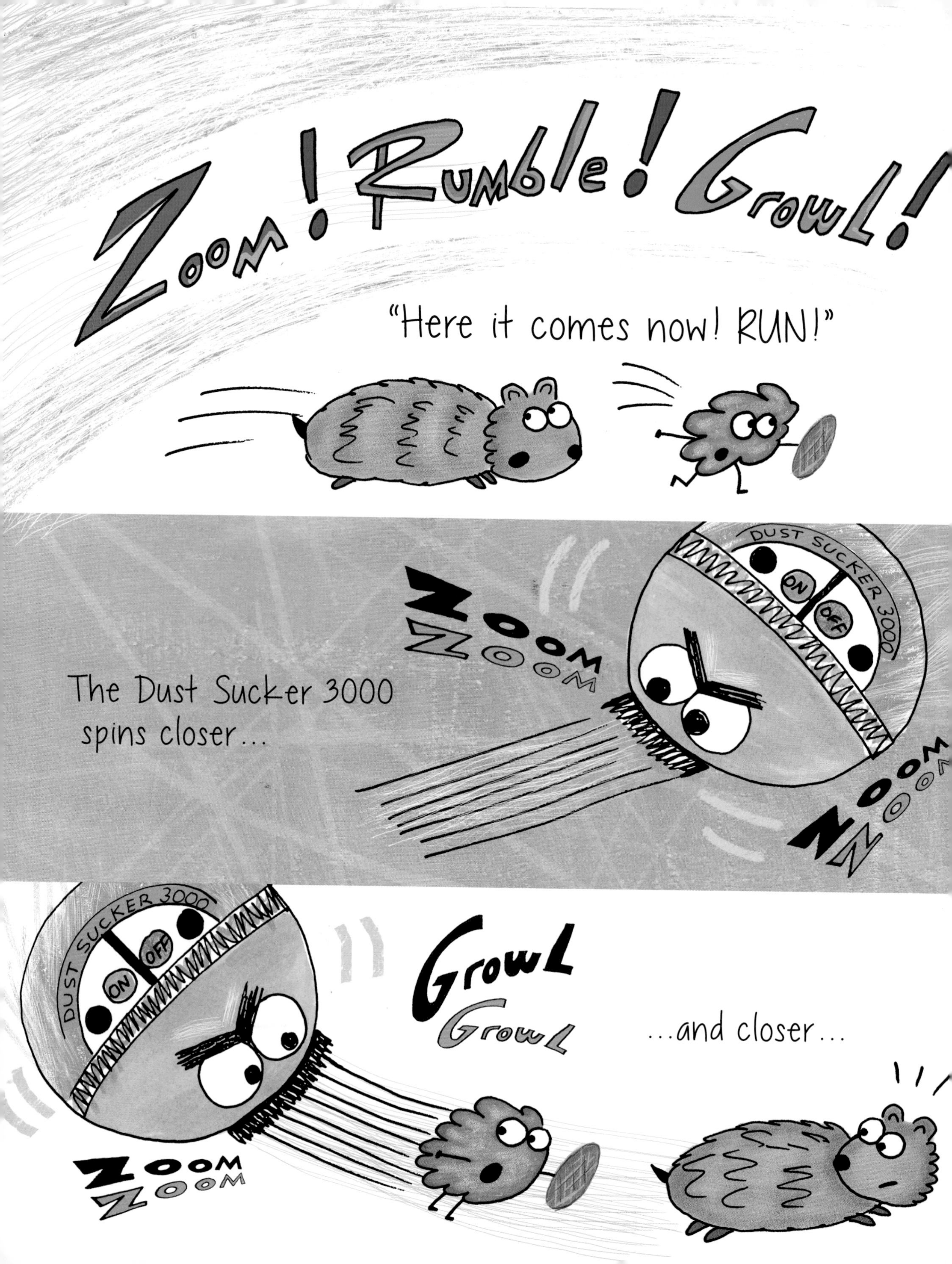
Zoom! Rumble! Growl!
"Here it comes now! RUN!"
DUST SUCKER 3000
ON
OFF
ZOOM ZOOM
The Dust Sucker 3000 spins closer...
ZOOM ZOOM
DUST SUCKER 3000
ON
OFF
Growl Growl
...and closer...
ZOOM ZOOM

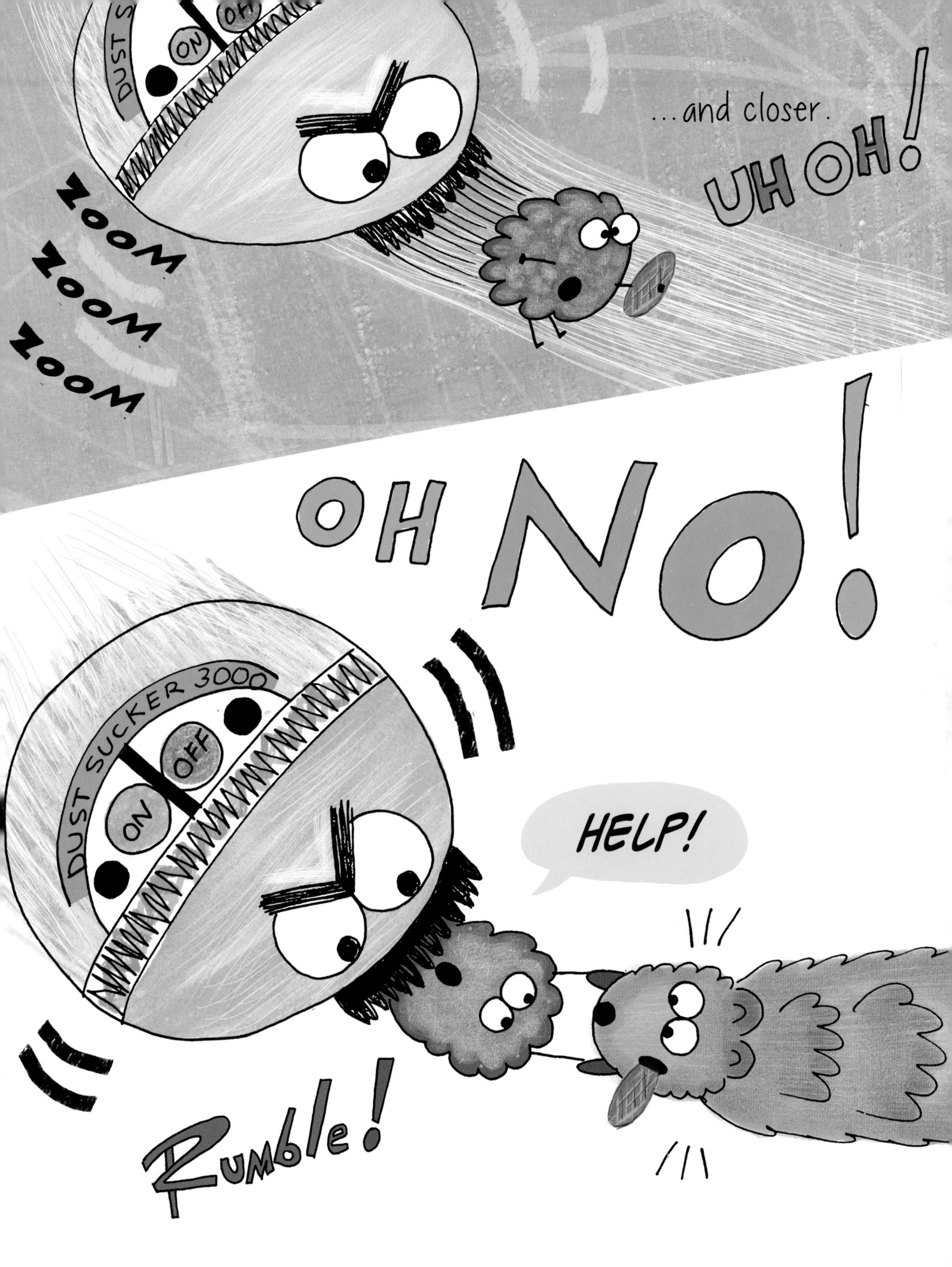
...and closer.
UH OH!
ZOOM
ZOOM
ZOOM
OH NO!
DUST SUCKER 3000
ON
OFF
HELP!
Rumble!

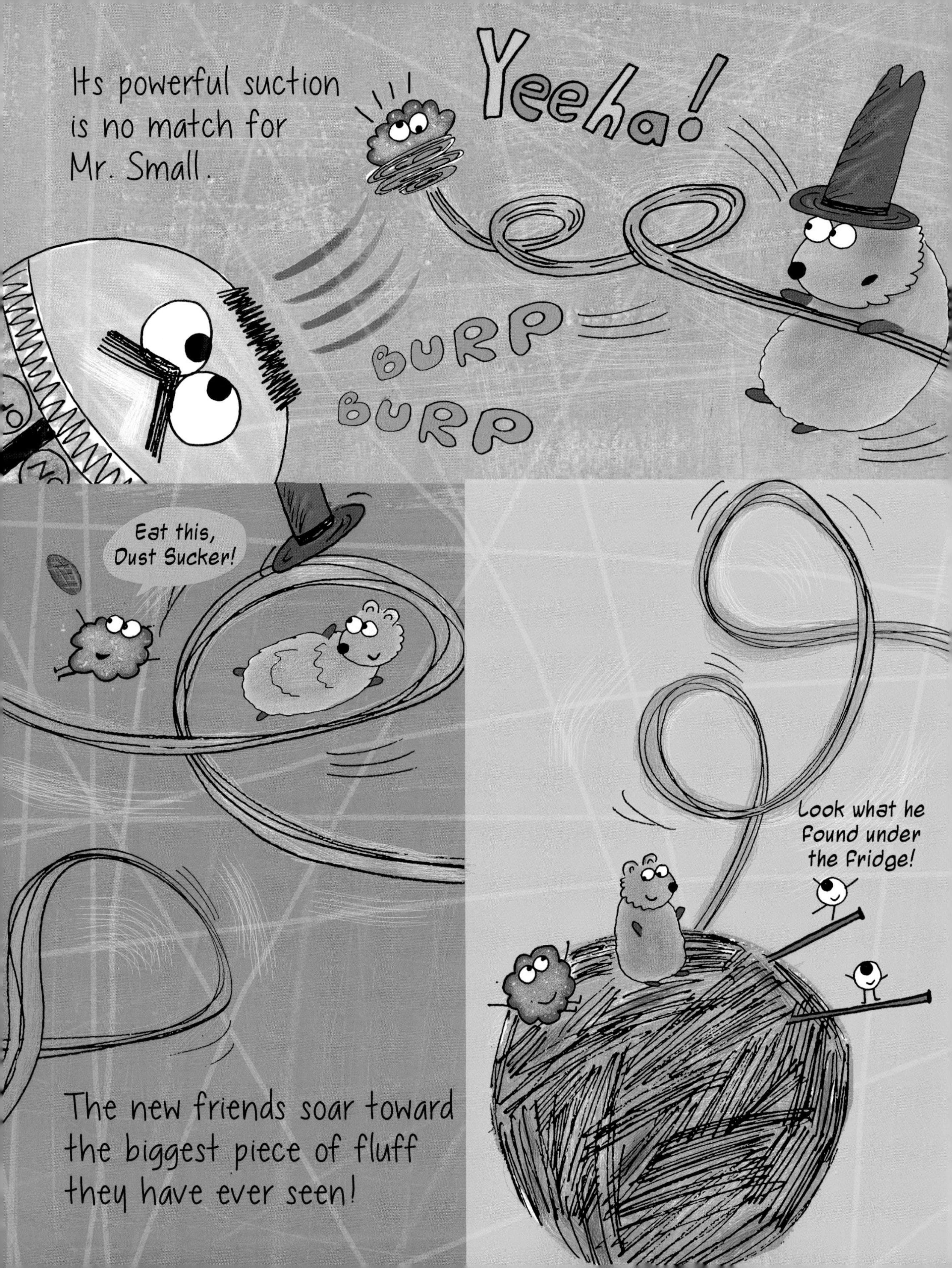
Its powerful suction is no match for Mr. Small.
Yeeha!
BURP
BURP
Eat this, Dust Sucker!
The new friends soar toward the biggest piece of fluff they have ever seen!
Look what he found under the fridge!

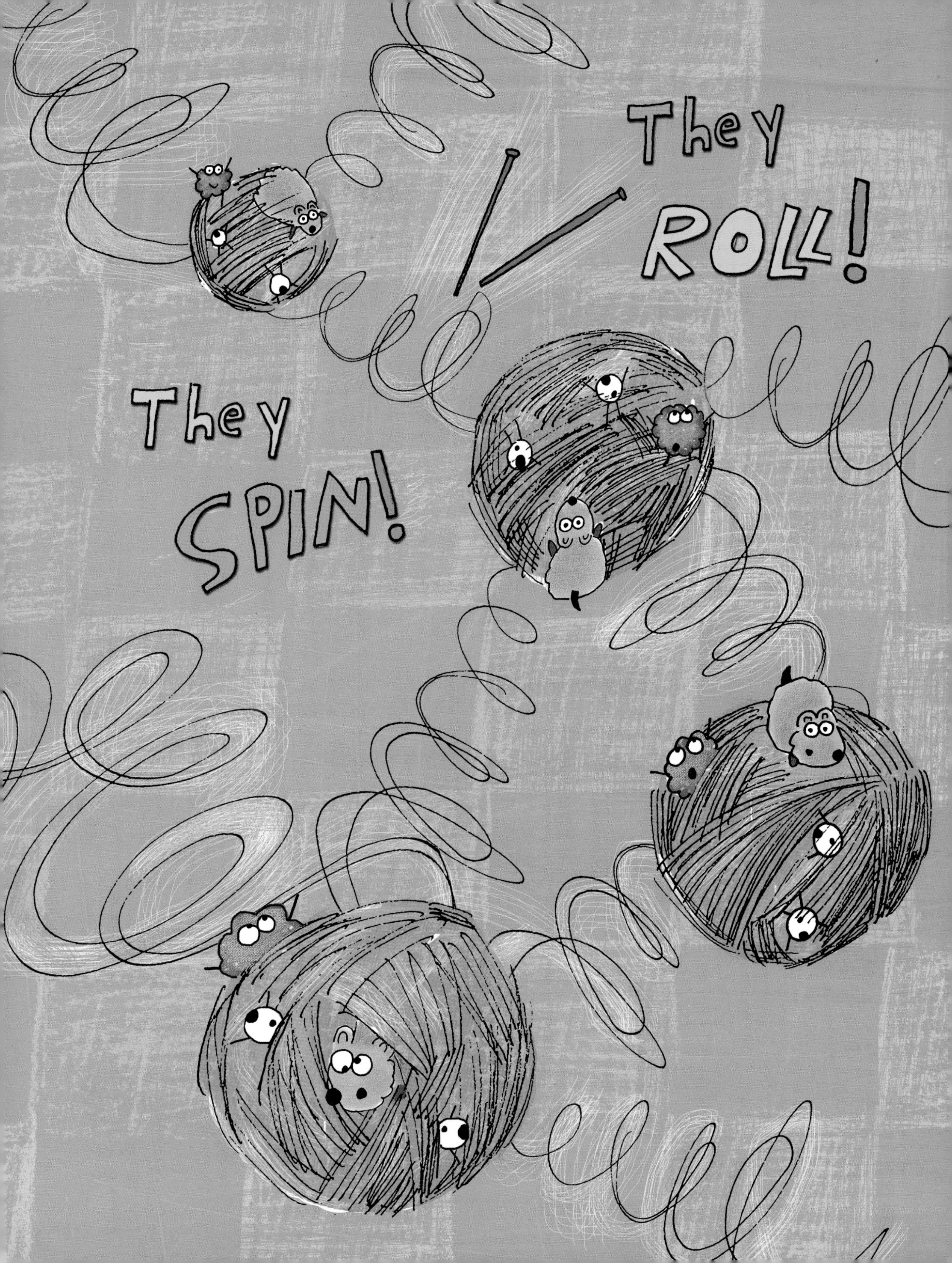
They ROLL!
They SPIN!

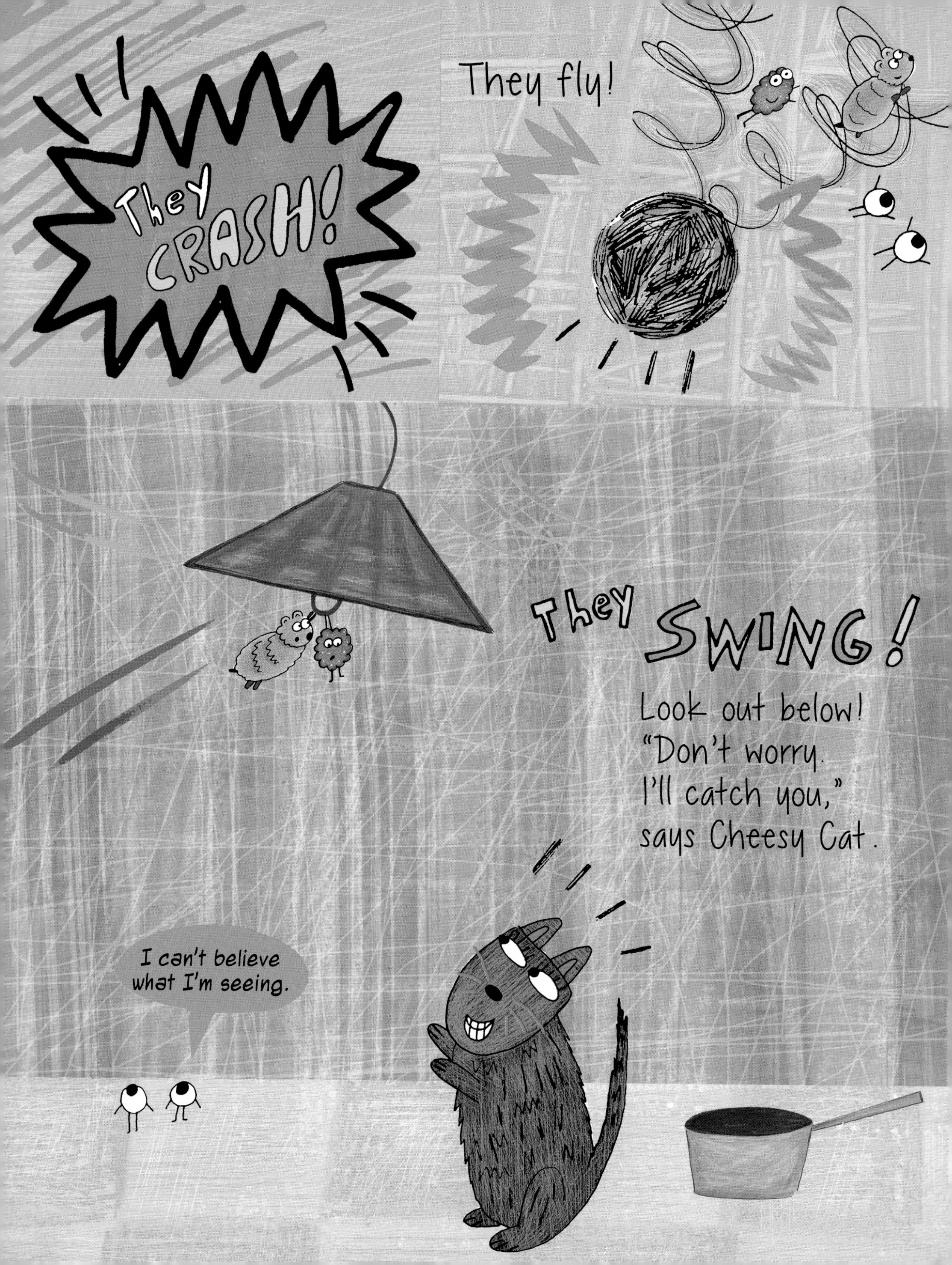
They CRASH!
They fly!
They SWING!
Look out below!
"Don't worry.
I'll catch you,"
says Cheesy Cat.
I can't believe what I'm seeing.

Mr. Small and his new
friend can't hang on!

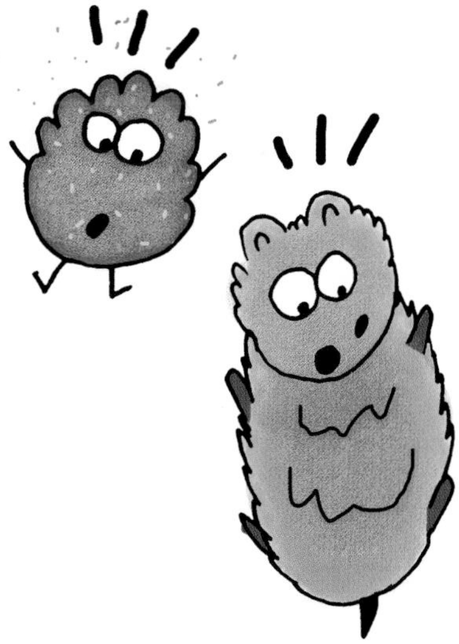

OH NO!

Will this be
the

END

of Mr. Small and Big Dusty?

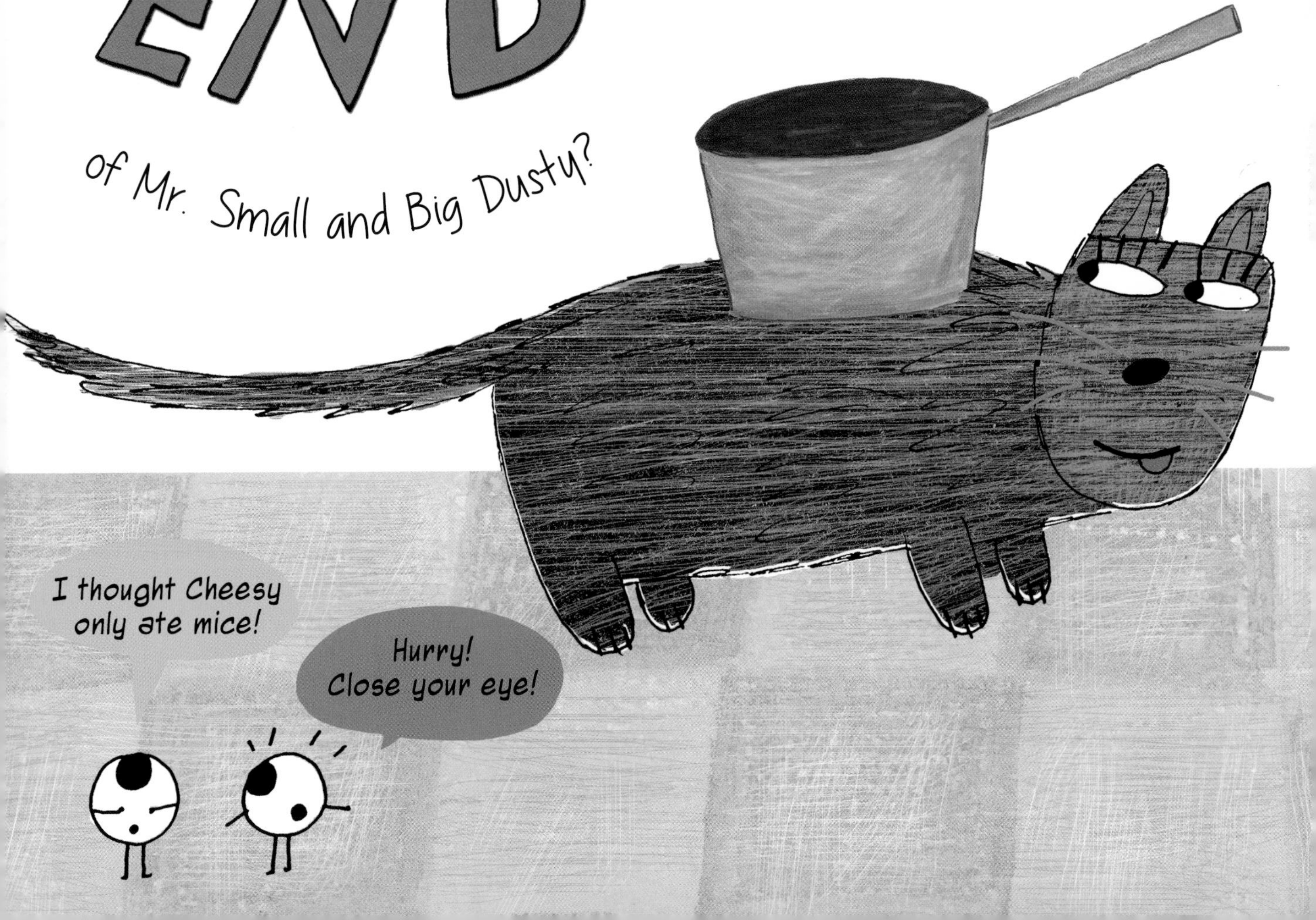
I thought Cheesy only ate mice!
Hurry! Close your eye!

Cheesy Cat grins and says, "Gotcha!"
Mr. Small is a quick thinking rodent.
"I've got something for you."
"For me?" asks Cheesy.

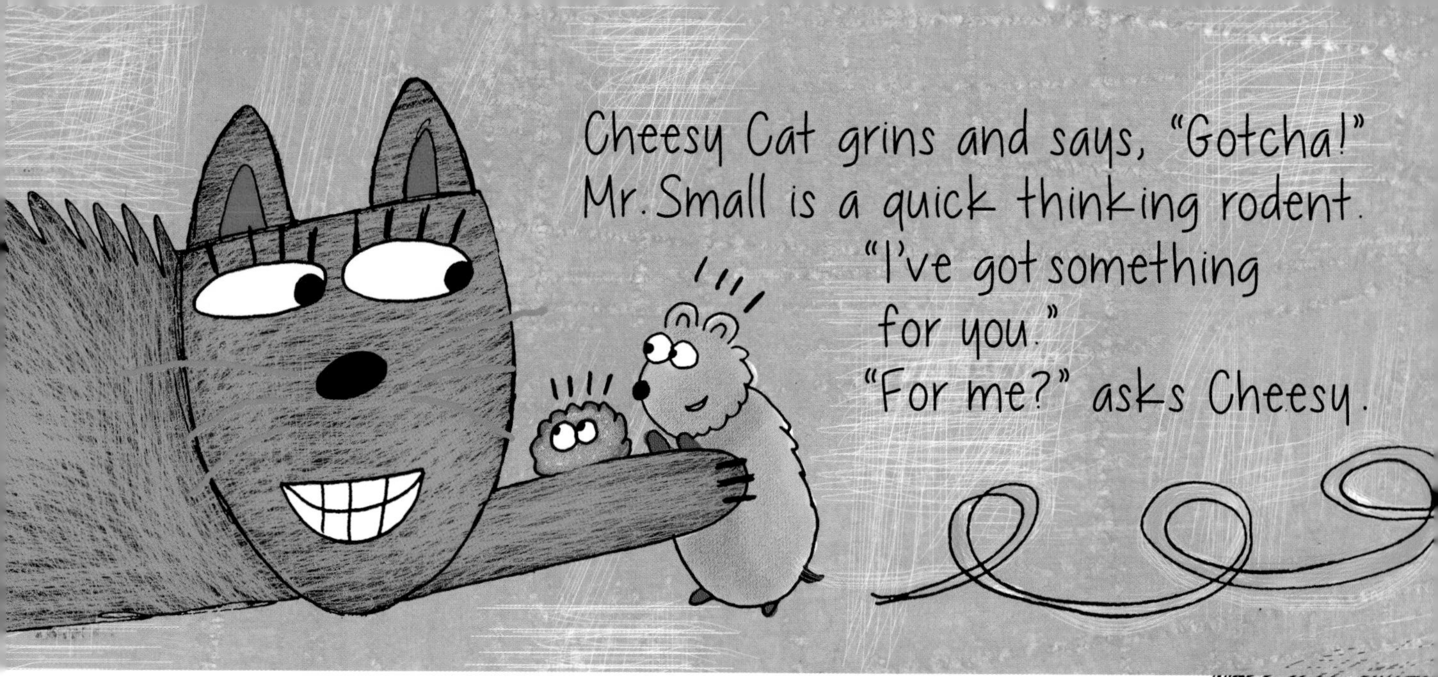

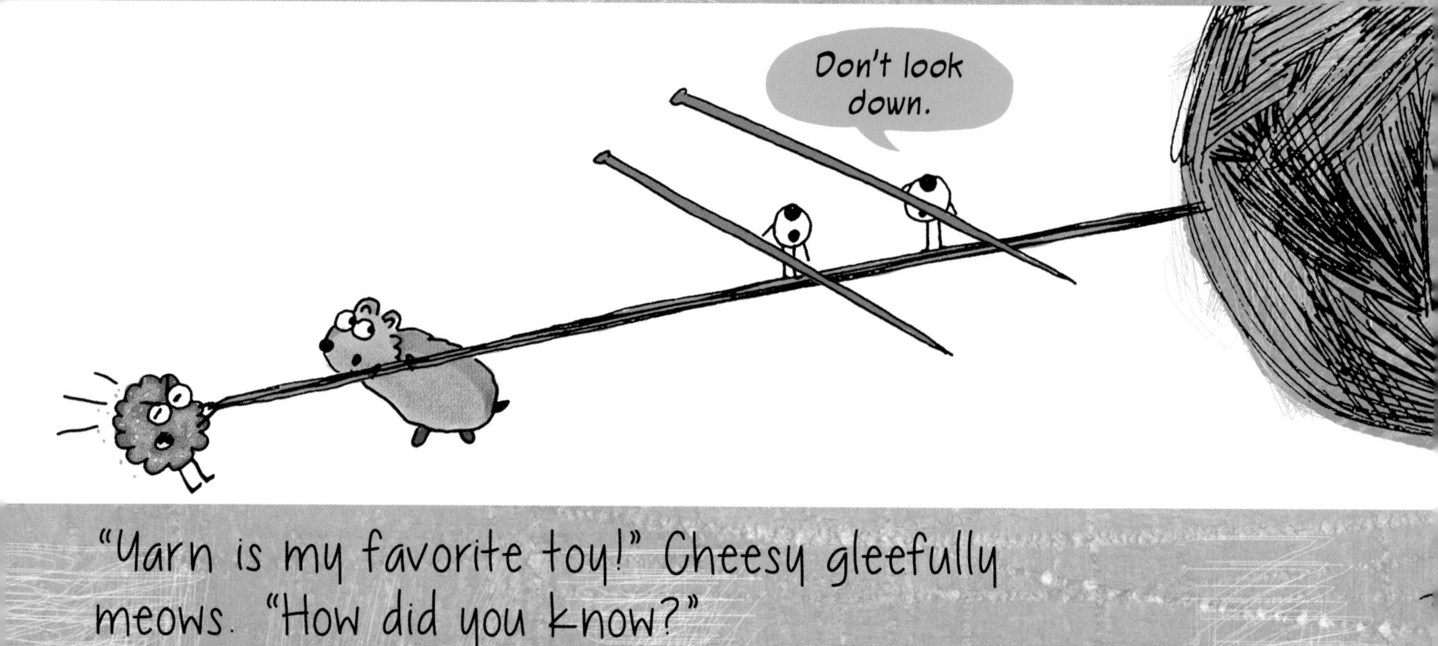
Don't look down.

"Yarn is my favorite toy!" Cheesy gleefully meows. "How did you know?"
"Lucky guess," says Mr. Small.
But our little friends are not safe for long!

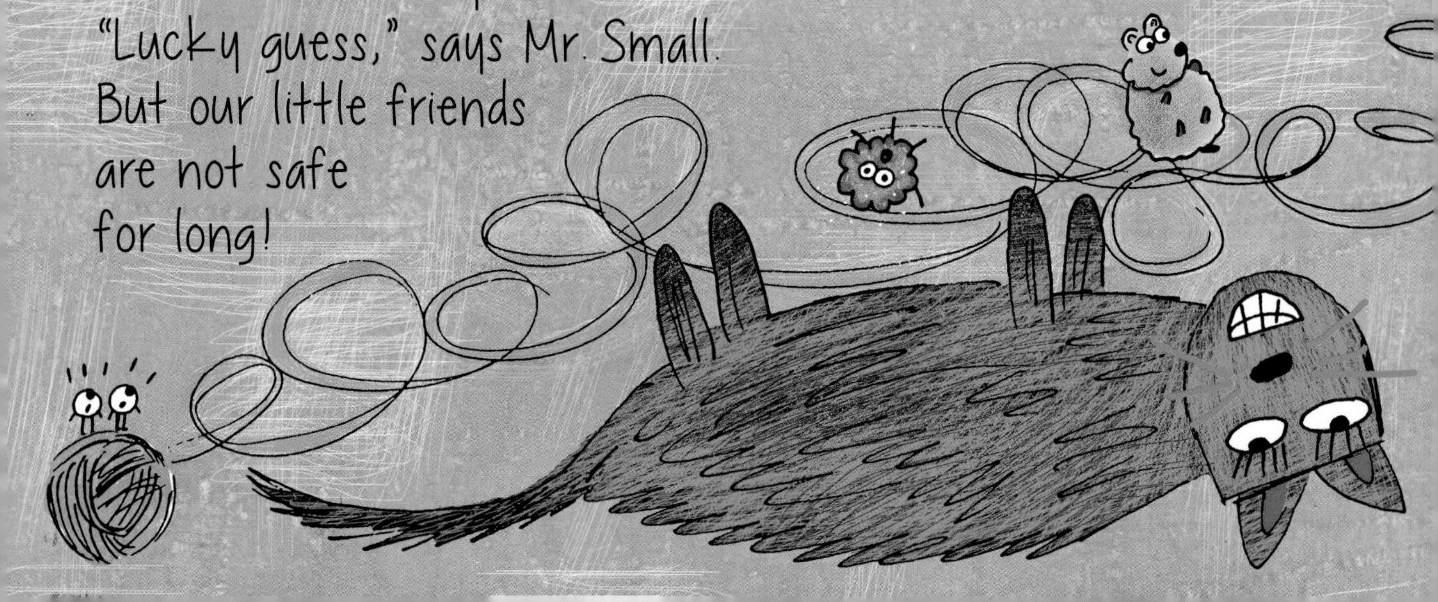

"Oh no!" yelps Big Dusty. "It's the Dust Sucker 3000 again!"

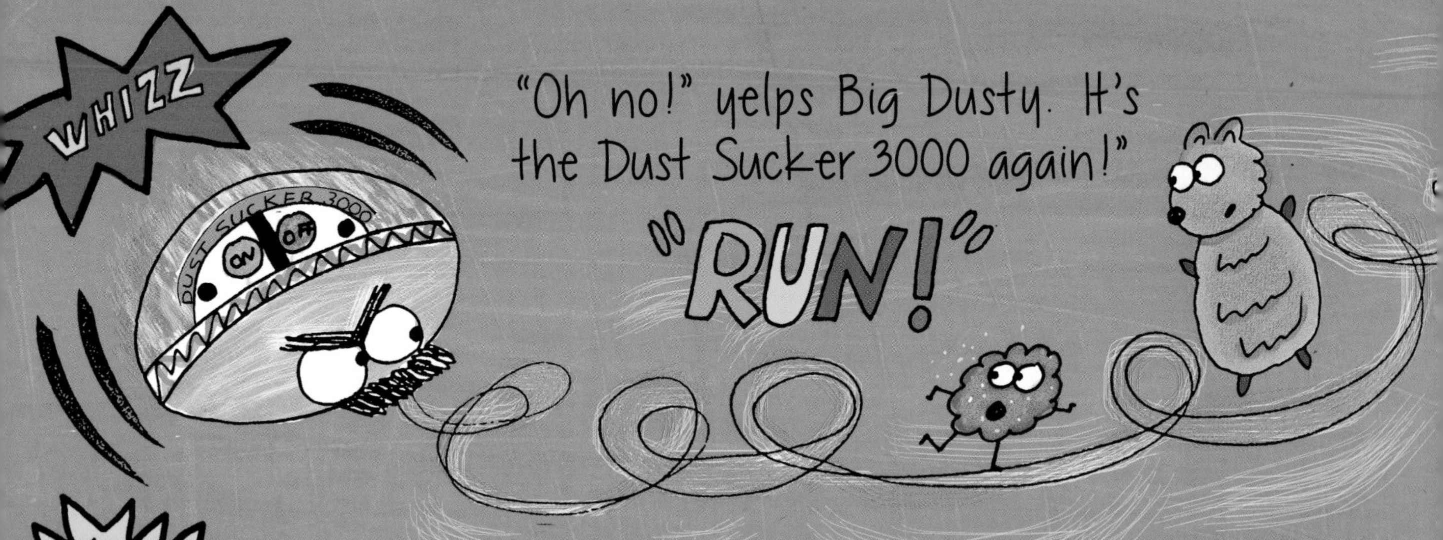
WHIZZ
DUST SUCKER 3000
ON
OFF
"RUN!"

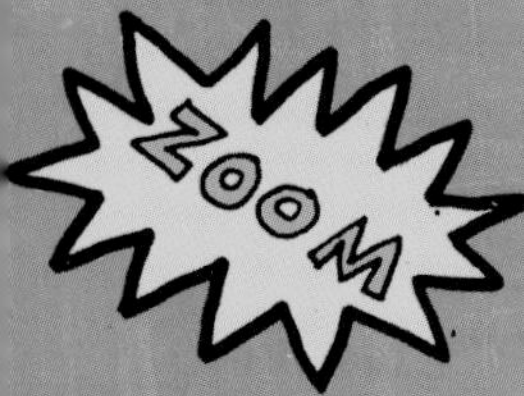
ZOOM

"I'm not afraid of that silly thing," growls Mr. Small. "Ready! Set! JUMP!"

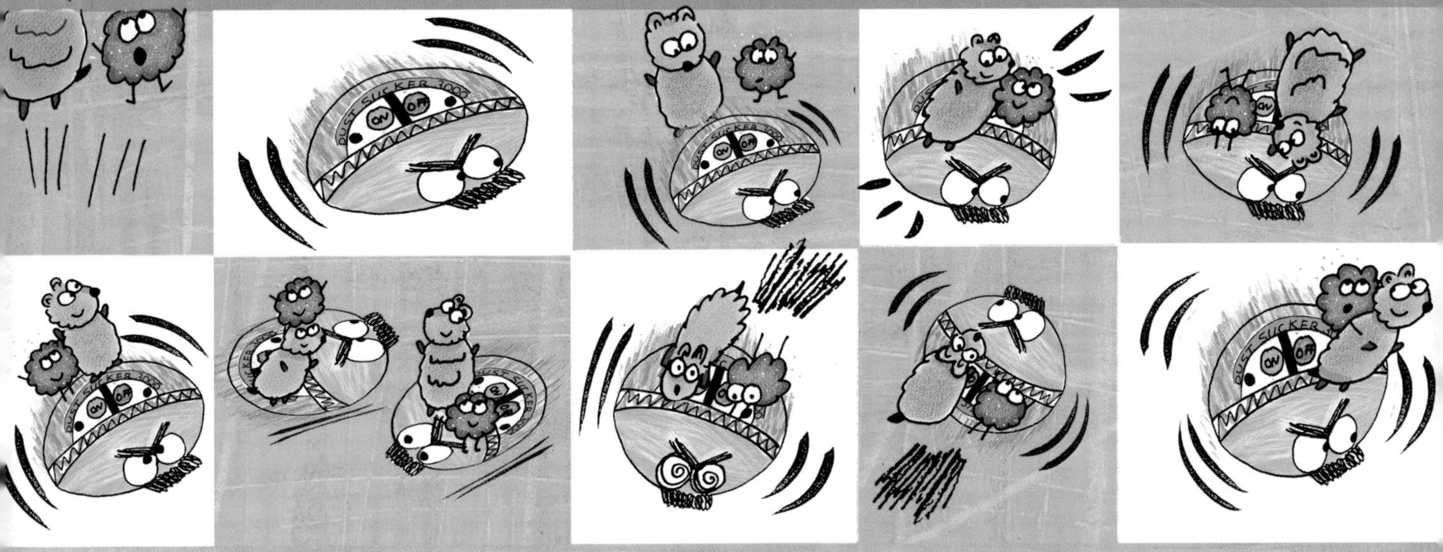
DUST SUCKER 3000
ON
OFF

"This is our stop, Big Dusty," shouts Mr. Small.

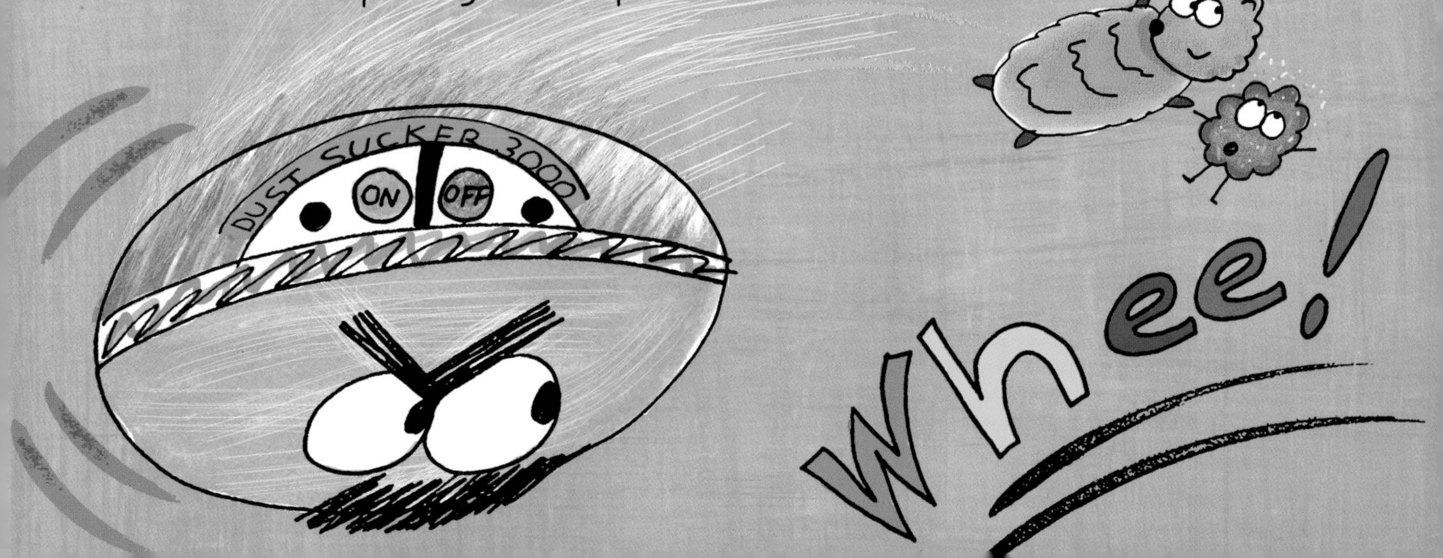
DUST SUCKER 3000
ON
OFF
Whee!

"Where do you live?" asks Mr. Small.

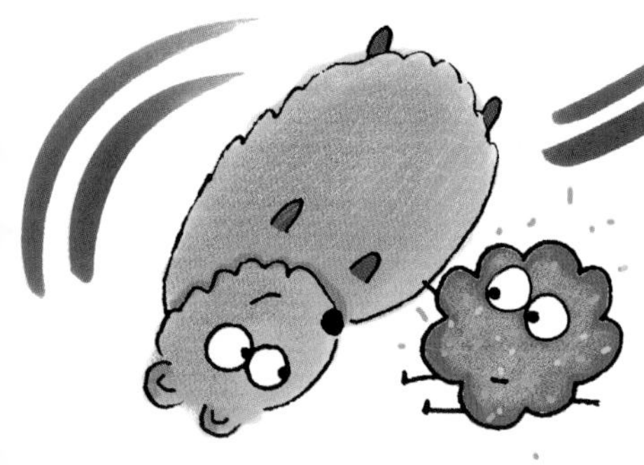

"Under the refrigerator," sighs Big Dusty. "That's the place for dust."

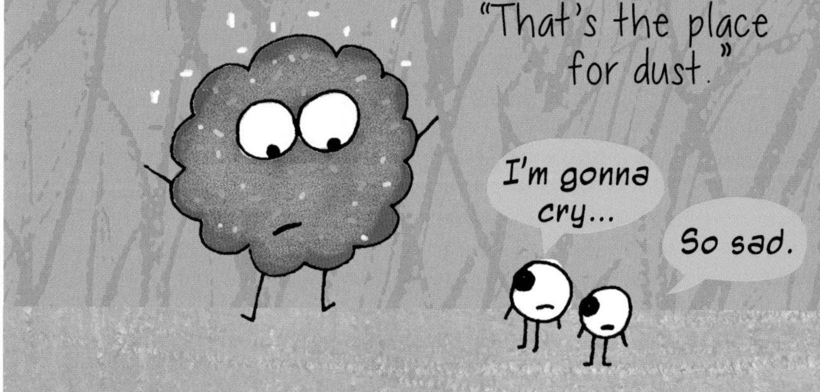
I'm gonna cry...
So sad.

"Not anymore!" says Mr. Small. "From now on you are going to live with me!"
"Hooray!" squeals Big Dusty.

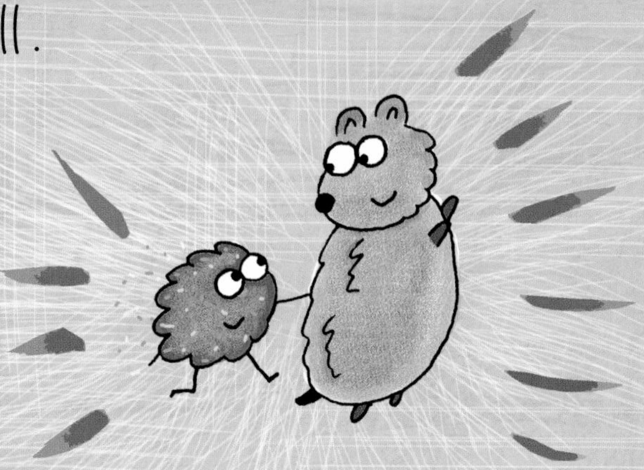

Teeny tiny hamsters love big adventures but it is always good to be back home safe and sound.

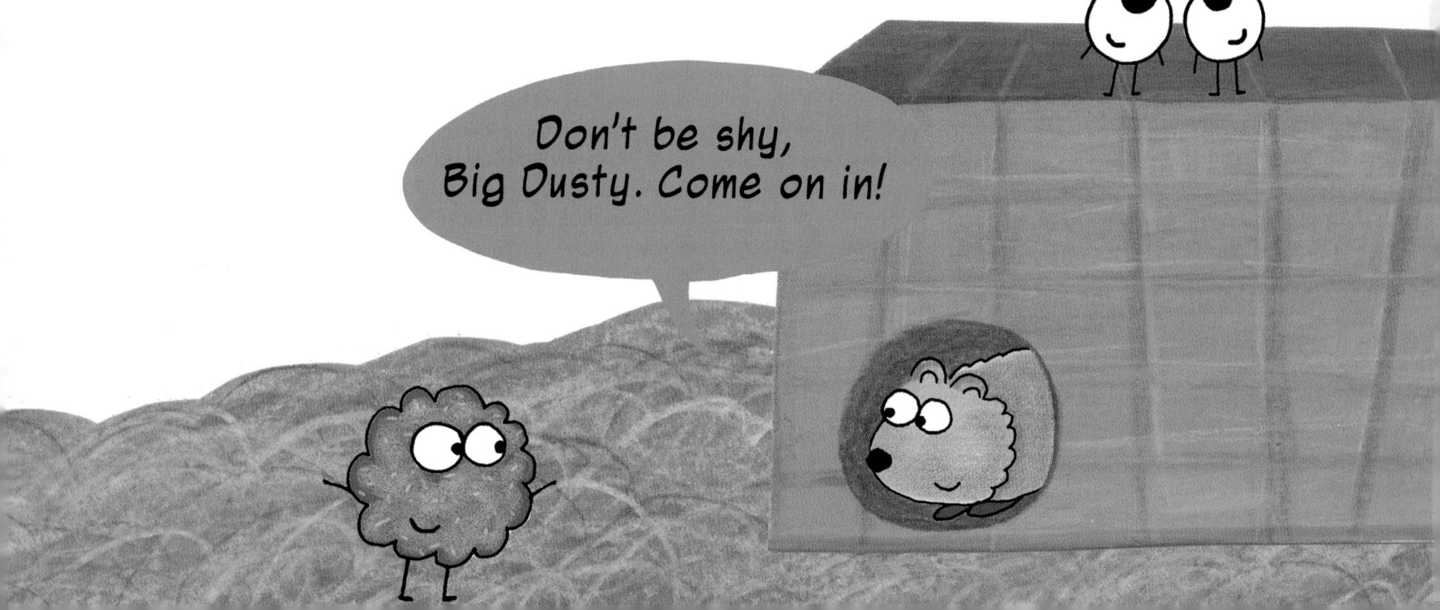
Don't be shy, Big Dusty. Come on in!

Big Dusty gets a warm welcome from the cozy fluff and bits of food.

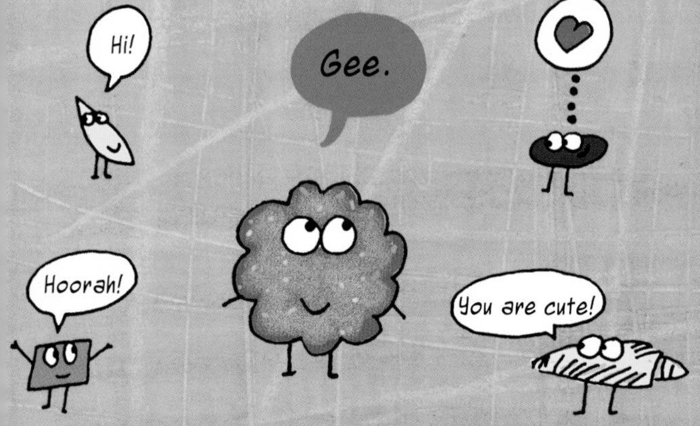
Hi!
Gee.
Hoorah!
You are cute!

AHHHH...

Mr. Small tucks in Big Dusty. "Sweet dreams," he says. "Sleep tight, Mr. Small," whispers Big Dusty.

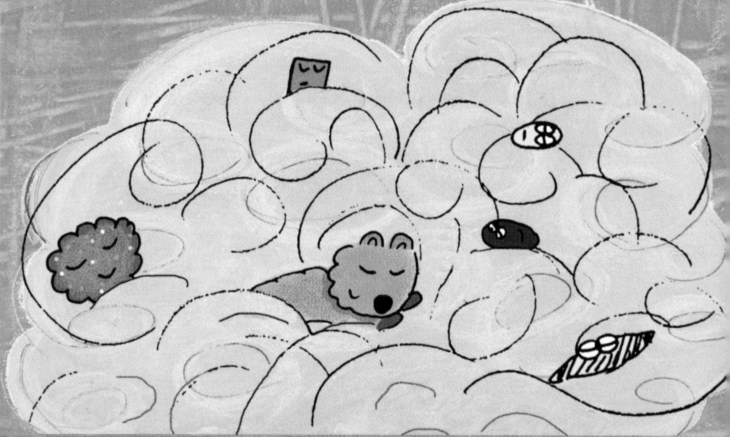

OH NO!

Poor Mr. Small. He wakes with a start. He still has one more adventure left. What could it be?

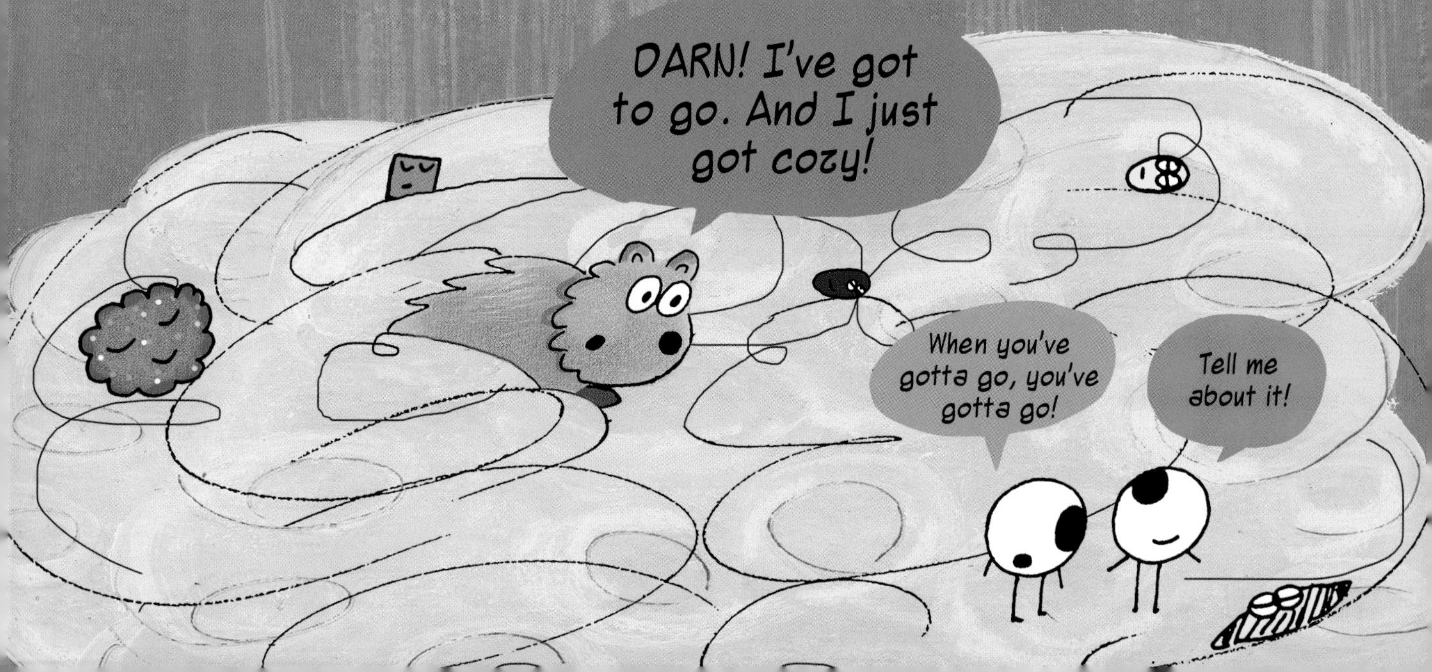
DARN! I've got to go. And I just got cozy!
When you've gotta go, you've gotta go!
Tell me about it!

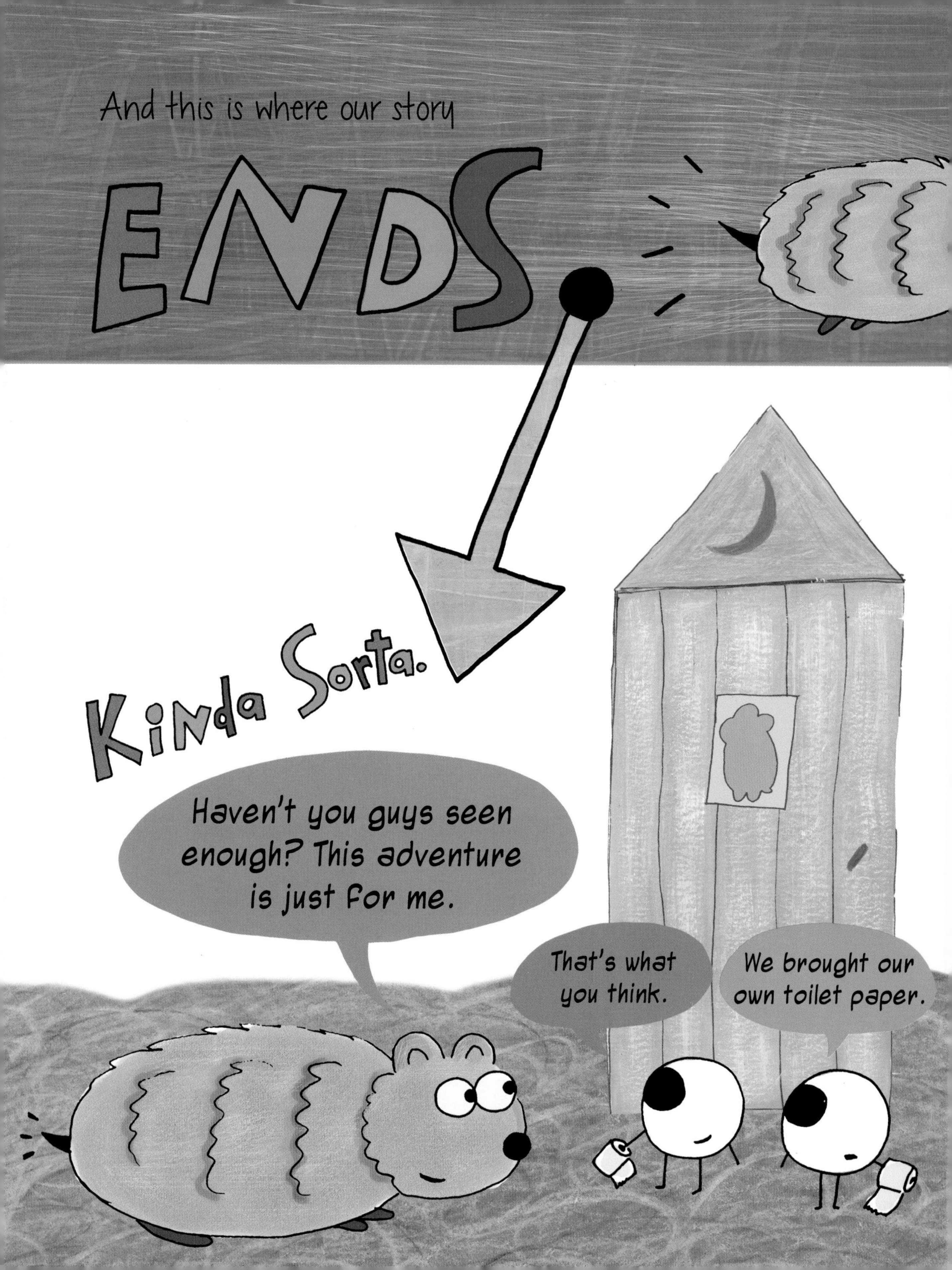
And this is where our story
ENDS.
Kinda Sorta.
Haven't you guys seen enough? This adventure is just for me.
That's what you think.
We brought our own toilet paper.